Printed in the United States of America

First Printing, 2018

ISBN-10 1976828198
ISBN-13 978-1976828195

Kindle Direct Publishing
123 Mesa Street
Scottsdale, AZ 00000

DEFY

KAYLEIGH GALLAGHER

Malo periculosam,
libertatem quam quietam servitutem
"I prefer dangerous freedom
over peaceful slavery."
-Thomas Jefferson-

Thank you to
all my friends and family who
helped me through the
writing process.

CONTENTS

PROLOGUE

The world was in chaos, thrown out of its balance at last.

The planet had been torn in two by war. Unending war; a growl from the depths of the human soul, a hunger for violence, a thirst for blood that could never be quenched. Humanity had always had a dark side, a cruelty that lusted for other lives spilled out on the floor. But never, not once in history, not even in the fifth world war, had it ever had such an opportunity. Such an ability. The population dwindled at a rapid rate as neither man nor animal was spared.

The atmosphere was ripped from its place, eaten alive by fire that suffocated the sky and smothered the air.

And yet no one ceased. No one stopped fighting, not as whirlwinds exploded into being, not as infants and children perished without need, not at the storms and tsunamis of Earth dying.

New technologies allowed nations to blast each other into oblivion. The oceans were stained brown and red from the pollution and blood that tainted its once pristine shores.

The ground was cracked in two from earthquakes, acid rain pouring down and stripping the trees of their leaves. Nuclear explosions that made the ground shudder caused staggering volcanic eruptions.

Mountains split into pieces, tons of solid rock sliding down into steep ravines.

Lady Liberty had fallen. The Eiffel Tower was bent in half. The Great Wall of China crumbled into nothingness. The Taj Mahal was incinerated. Famous landmarks, precious heritage, treasured culture, reduced to ashes as humanity dared itself to go one step further.

The year was 3004.

And only twelve were still safe. Underground. Separated from everyone.

They called themselves the Founders.

They had just reached the decision to allow humanity to live, with a set of conditions. Laws that set up a careful boundary, never to be broken, between humans and nature. Laws that ensured safety for the entire planet.

Or so they thought.

As they waited for the tremors to cease, for it to be safe to ascend to the ground above at last, no one noticed the girl shrouded in shadows.

Her eyes burned with hate.

CHAPTER 1

Do not fight.

That was the first rule of the Code. The second was that schoolchildren were not allowed in the residential area. The third was that no children could seek their birth parents, and no parents could seek their children. Any displays of greed resulted in the week's rations cut in half.

The rules went on and on. Failure to obey was violently punished. Everyone had the same house, the same clothes, the same amount of money.

Everyone went to schools built the same way, walking in neat, straight rows, always on the right side of the hallway. There was a rotating schedule of who sat with who at lunch. Lunchtime and Homeroom were times of silence, of work, preparing for the day.

Socializing on a personal level was not allowed. Stiff, formal greetings were exchanged, and then the rest of the day was carried out. At age twenty-five, one was assigned a spouse with whom they would have children, who were sent to the Raising Centers, and then return to their normal lives.

Alone.

Each Pair was allowed up to two children. If one had twins, those were their two. If somebody had more than two children, the extra babies were killed on the spot. One was allowed two weeks with these children, to give them assigned names from a list that was cycled through, and to nurse them until they were old enough to be taken away without any memory of the parents who didn't love them.

Everyone was the same. A clone in a regulated life that no one could control, incapable of uniqueness, of emotion.

I was different, defiant.

Defective.

In the Conurbation, *Defective* meant *dangerous*. It meant *death*.

Of course, it wouldn't be official until my seventeenth birthday, when the Elders entered my head and examined my mind, deeming whether I was fit for society. For routine.

No one knew what I was yet except for the Raisers assigned to me.

Maybe it was when I refused to wear the uniform. A pleated gray skirt, a long-sleeved, gray collared blouse, knee-high gray socks, gray flats. My hair in a tight, high ponytail.

Maybe it was when I took my hair out of the ponytail and let it fall, a straight curtain, to my elbows. That had been the first time it'd been down for longer than the time it took to change it from the two pigtails that the Fledgling girls wore. Maybe it was then.

Or maybe it was when I ducked out of the line; when I got in an argument; when I smashed a school window because I was so, so angry. Possibly, it was when I received a deep cut on my arm as a marker of my disobedience and the next day it was gone.

Maybe it was then.

Perhaps it was just my appearance; my atypically slanted eyes, my high, sharp cheekbones, my rounded ears that tapered to delicate points, my freakishly pale skin and straight black hair. People often told me I was beautiful, but the term they used more often was *strange*. I was required to wear layers of unflattering makeup and brown hair dye to hide my unsettling beauty, until I was eighteen, when I would get gene therapy. I hadn't gone a single day without the cosmetics since I was thirteen.

No matter when I stood out, or how, no one knew. No one knew, and no one could know. Because Defects like me were killed in the Finding, a week before the Coming of Age ceremony.

Five years ago, my Raisers spoke in a hushed voice. I don't remember exactly what they'd said, but the gist of it was I was going to die.

I had been eleven.

Now the day of my seventeenth birthday was just a month away.

I had two options: run and let the Jurisprudents catch me or accept my fate. Both involved me dying. I couldn't decide yet which would be more painful.

I stopped on my way to my desk, staring at a piece of neat, lined paper someone had left there while I was in the bathroom.

if it weren't for your Finding ceremony, I'd have liked to have your kids.

My lips tightened. I tore the paper from the desk and crumpled it into a tight ball, jamming it in the trash can.

No one would need to use *that* again.

"Karen," came my teacher's appraising voice. Wasting paper was wrong.

At the tight, disapproving faces of my classmates, my face grew hot.

"I'm sorry, madam," I apologized, wishing I could kick something.

I forced my attention back to the front of the dull slate room before I could get in more trouble, where the teacher was showing artifacts from the Dark Ages, when none of the rules that kept us safe were in place. Glowing blue photographs floated nearby, information scrawled beside each picture. We used to have these items, and I knew most of them by heart, but the Conurbation had taken them, stripped them away until there was nothing left but concepts and memories.

The holograms displayed weapons, *so* many weapons, designed to hurt and kill and intimidate.

A physical manifestation of today's digital books, but instead of just science and math and history, instead of just storing data, they included unnecessary fallacies called "fiction." Fiction was proven to poison the minds of young children, wasting their time with lies about things and places and people that didn't exist.

Samples of class notes, where everyone had their own handwriting, no two the same, and the names were just as fickle.

Sketches and paintings, foreign words that meant *making images*.

13

Photographs, which showed people who looked *different* from each other, unique. The groups had a discordant feel, like too many voices talking at once, shards of glass that didn't fit right.

There was a girl who had shaved her entire head. A boy who was covered in colorful displays from his neck down. A teen with at least six piercings lining each ear. Layered bobs, patterns shaved into a buzz cut, black hair on one half, white hair on the other, threadbare jeans, shredded shirts, it went on and on. I saw belly-baring shirts and elaborate dresses, tank tops emblazoned on the front, dyed bangs, so much color my eyes hurt.

Then we got to the tragedies.

People standing out on marble stairs, holding signs that proclaimed their dissent, fighting for things that were already theirs. A woman curled up on the ground as a group of men kicked her in the back.

"There were five world wars before the First Death of Earth," the hologram told us in a not-unpleasant monotone, black-and-white photos flashing death counts and bloody photographs. Scandals, murder, battle scenes and torture weapons. I saw people starving on the streets and killing each other to get what they wanted. They said they were free.

This was truly a flawed society, a society without equality, without balance.

It was imperfect, but hopeful, at least in my opinion.

So as the rest of the class recoiled, disgusted, I thought maybe the Dark Ages were heaven.

CHAPTER 2

The Conurbation did not appreciate complexity.

Complexity was me in a word.

I had two sets of clothing. One was my school uniform, that boring gray outfit that made me look like everyone else in the world. The other was my sleepwear. It consisted of a pair of knee-length, loose linen shorts, gray, along with a baggy gray, short sleeved top. Despite the sweltering heat of the Conurbation, these garments were long, designed to be "conservative" and "prudent."

There were four classes of school: Preliminary, Primary, Secondary, and Tertiary. There were five years in each school besides Tertiary, which had two to five years, depending upon the extent of a student's final education. School lasted nine hours, from seven to four, Sunday through Friday. Children began education at two, and the most educated, like Medicals or Jurisprudents, ended their schooling three years before they were to be married, at age twenty-two. It was around this time that they were assigned a suitable partner based on the magnitude of their edification and their sparse personalities. I was in my fourth year of Secondary.

My room in the Raising Center was small and square and polished stone, with a single gray bed that had simple white linen sheets, mounted on the wall. A table was positioned on either side of the bed, gray and cube shaped.

The large hexahedron with a small area for me to put my legs served as a desk, with a padded, white chair for me to sit in.

A hologram device received all my assignments and study material. The lights were set to go out at nightfall. I had a small orb that emanated pale white luminescence for one hour after sunset so I could review my history and math courses. I was taught reading and writing, of course, but there weren't many books for me to read, and writing was unnecessary unless you were the Secretary. Writing sparked creativity, and imagination was a crime, if ever considered to be put to use.

If I weren't Defective, I would have liked to be Secretary. The Secretary had access to all the records in the Conurbation. Every person ever born into this society, every Defect, every Rogue, and every leader. All those people. Their names, birth dates, times of death, parents, siblings. Their stories.

When I was younger, I thought I could find out who my parents were, and if I had any blood brothers or sisters, despite the strict law against it.

I remembered taking a trip in the first year of Secondary to the Record Halls. We didn't get to go anywhere or touch anything. We just looked at it. So I "accidentally" got separated from the group and unintentionally wandered toward the Defects and Rogues. I accessed one of the files and pulled out identification holos at random to read them.

The only way to distinguish between two people were their identifications. These consisted of the first initial of their name, along with their number, the sole thing that set each person apart. My ID was K-9735, because I was the nine thousand, seven hundred thirty-fifth citizen of the Conurbation.

The first one I found was a girl with dirty blonde hair, splotched with the mandatory brown dye she'd probably washed out, pulled back into a ponytail and wild blue eyes. Something about her was a little crazed and a little dangerous, and she shot a cheeky grin into the camera. Her ID was A-9738. The holo read *Name: Ava 9738. Born: Rotation 12, Year 4517 AFD. Status: Rogue.* That was as far as I got before the card blanked out. *Error*, read the new message. *Information not found.* I slid it back to its place, fighting the flash of irritation that could get me killed.

The next was a girl with jet-black hair and piercing blue eyes with an odd brownish stripe down the middle of one of them. I read it quickly, not wanting to miss out on the information. *E-9737. Name: Elizabeth 9737. Born: Rotation 9, year 4517 AFD. Status: Rogue. Infractions: Repeated Break-Ins. Black Marketing. Insubordination. Detention for Drawing in Class. Executed: 4534, Aged 17. Body destroyed.* Then the card went blank again, flashing the same message from before. I stared at it for a long moment. Zoe was executed in 4534... that was four years from now.

I-8837. Isabel. Rotation 14, 4302 AFD. Defect. Disabled Security Cameras. Hacked into Knowledge Archive. Ashes contained for genetic research. I stared at the long-gone girl with the scared green eyes and curly red hair for a long moment, swallowing hard. That could have been me, could still be me.

N-9729. Nathan. Rotation 3, 4513 AFD. Rogue. Commandeered Pistol. Shattered Senate Windows. Aggravated Assault on Governor and 4 Secondary Students. Sent to Juvenile 8 Times. There was an option to scroll down and view more of his crimes, but I ignored it. *Executed 4530, Aged 14. Body destroyed.* The blond-haired teenager

19

glowered into the camera, his hair just marginally longer than was allowed. His eyes were an angry, fierce blue color, and he looked like he wanted to break something with his bare hands. There was one other thing I noticed, for his head was tilted almost imperceptibly to the side. His ears were somewhat pointed, like mine.

M-9713. Matthew. Rotation 2, 4513 AFD. Rogue. Detention for Stealing Teacher's Lesson Plans. Assaulted 6 Students on Separate Occasions. Hospitalized 4 Senators. Vandalism. Sent to Juvenile 2 Times. Sent to Correction 3 Times. Record of Execution Destroyed. Executed 4530, Aged 17. Body destroyed. This boy had warm brown eyes and stark, naturally brown hair, with the ghost of a shy smile around his mouth. In his picture, his shoulders were slumped and his gaze downcast, a defeated air about him. He looked for all the world like he was on his way to die, which, according to his record, he was.

Oliver. Rogue. Dead.

Ava. Defect. Dead.

Mia. Rogue. Dead.

Thomas. Defect. Dead.

Jacqueline. Rogue. Dead. I paused on this name. It was none I had ever heard before, and uncommon names were illegal. How interesting. She had a thin, dark face with prominent cheekbones and honey blonde hair, cool brown eyes and a frosty look about her. As she glowered into the camera, one hand grasped her arm, I saw just how skinny she was, bones jutting through her skin. *Infractions. Vandalism. Property Damage. Executed 4533, Aged 17.*

Even at that age, and even with the glitches and the inaccuracies, I'd known there was little to no chance that these Rogues were still alive. Maybe these holos were all that was left of them.

I slid the card back.

A file in my periphery caught my attention; it was newer-looking and labeled with the word *Aberration*. I stood, curling my fingers around the handle, about to pull it open.

"K-9735!"

A firm hand planted itself on my shoulder. I stiffened and turned to meet the disdainful eyes of my teacher. My stomach plummeted.

"Five hours detention, Karen. I wish I could say I expected more."

Now I shook myself out of my daze, pulled out a tablet, and pressed the silver button on the side. A blue, floating image appeared before me. It was a map of the Conurbation, next to its Code of laws.

"History of the Conurbation," droned the deep, slow male voice— again, not unpleasant, just *boring*. "Human greed destroyed

21

civilization from the inside. Eradicating human jealousy was the first mission of the new Conurbation. Order was established in the chaos and–"

The voice blurred a little.

My eyes slid shut.

I was standing on a hill.

Thunder flashed. People were running and screaming.

Explosive noise in rapid succession. Deep, rattling booms.

A girl stood before me. She had rounded, chin length black hair with blue streaks. Enormous blue eyes. Thin lips. A tiny, upturned nose with a splash of freckles on her cheeks. A black jumpsuit covered her like a sheath. She was angry, the air crackling around her to demonstrate her wrath. She glared down at me, leaning in close.

"This," she hissed, jabbing a finger at the fire and fear and screaming and death. "This is all your fault. I could have stopped this if it weren't for your kind. You owe me now. You owe me."

She pulled back and smiled.

"By the way, my name is Astris." Her smile grew warm, welcoming. An unsettling change in emotion from just seconds earlier. "And I need a few favors."

CHAPTER 3

I had the pressing feeling on my chest of forgetting something important.

Weird flashes of memory swirled around me, attacking at unexpected moments. Sometimes a thought, sometimes a sensation or emotion. Phantom smoke clogged my nostrils, my chest constricted as the floor vanished beneath my feet. Then I blinked and it was gone.

I let out a tiny gasp, bracing my hands on the desk as *something* caressed my mind, the sharp scent of salt washing away the smoke. The cold tendril brushed past the wall around my thoughts, ancient and bitter.

"I need—"

There, the first half of a sentence, in a voice I did not recognize.

"—your kind—"

These words came with a splitting headache that stubbornly remained until I downed some pain meds and sat down on my bed.

I wasn't dressed yet and would likely be late to school this morning, but I still had some extra time to do something stupid, so I wrote my name.

Not the name I was assigned, but the name that was mine and mine alone.

And I did it using the wrong handwriting.

Karen. That was my name. That was how it was spelled. There was the handwriting that I, and everyone else, was supposed to use. Instead, I wrote *Raven*.

Raven.

And then, as an afterthought, I put *I am* in front of that, forming a sentence.

I am Raven.

It was stunning, how beautiful that name was, as if making it mine gave it new life.

I called myself this after the sleek, shiny black birds that stood watch outside Secondary, ancient black eyes filled with disgust, as though even they knew something was wrong. The words were scratchy and near illegible, but at least it was mine, and mine alone.

I am Raven.

Mine and mine alone.

I smiled, a small, secret thing, and slipped the piece of paper beneath my mattress.

Individuality is dangerous, said rule seventeen of the Code. Names are to be selected with permanence. Changing an assigned name is strictly prohibited.

And I understood. Agreed, even.

But I also didn't care.

And that was dangerous.

My port-holo beeped, alerting me to the arrival of my meal. It would contain a typical breakfast of oatmeal and vitamin supplements; or, if I was extra lucky and the chickens had done well that week, eggs.

I ignored it and sat at the desk.

The salty, ancient tendril brushed the walls of my mind again, urging, ordering. I pulled out my sharpened, government-issue pencil. It had a long, pale pink eraser and was covered in gray paint, except for the wood-and-graphite tip. Silver lettering declared it a number two pencil, officially approved by the Conurbation. And I began to draw.

It wasn't much. A city like mine, but this one was different.

When I looked out the window of my dorm, I saw dusty, desert roads, cracked and overgrown with weeds. The stark black they had once been were now pale gray and caked with sand, the bright yellow stripes painted down the middle faded to a musty cream color. Roads like these snaked through the city, devoid of life. They sprawled across the landscape until the borders. Sun- and wind-weathered buildings stretched across the terrain.

The city was organized in a circle, with a plus-shaped building at its heart. This was the Raising Center. I was in the East Wing, Sector 17, Room 45. From my view of the whole of the Conurbation, I could see the government buildings forming a square around the child-raising complex. Past the administrative buildings were the schools, in a tilted square around the government. Then was a circle of residential homes, three rings close together. A band of greenhouses and livestock structures followed, before the workshops and job centers. In the midst of this last area was a strip of the city left from before the First Death of Earth, the Forbidden Sector.

Greenhouses, coated in dust and dirt, grew the food and wood for the entire, 35,385-square-mile city. They were made of rusty metal, and overgrown with wild plants, strangled by each other and the dry heat.

The sandstone houses, organized by age and partnership status, had flat roofs and heavy iron doors that scraped open, screeching across stone floors. Each house was in a small "L" shape, allowing for three rooms: bedroom, kitchen, bathroom. Sparse lawns grew dead brown grass, sprinklers spraying filthy sewage, as though maybe that would help. Chain link fences separated each plot of land. At the edge of this residential area was the housing for Elders. From the clump of streets in the center of the city, the roads grew fewer and fewer, the ends of a tangled ball of thread. Ominous gray walls rose hundreds of feet above the abandoned desert roads, suffocating the air with reddish brown sand.

Only an idiot would try to escape.

Perhaps it would be wise to let us think we had a choice, make us believe we were free. But the Conurbation did not believe in lies. Break our hopes from the beginning, and we would never pose a threat to them. Break our dreams from the start, and we would always be slaves.

Ebony-black and iron-gray banners hung over the double doors of each school, advertising the Conurbation's slogan: *If You Feel the Burn, You Will Learn to fear the Flame.*

Flyers and graffiti — not yet removed — proclaimed unrest and rebellion; a defiant refusal to lay down and die. Just this morning one of the Execution Facilities went up in flames.

It was comforting to know that not everyone was happy — not everyone was the same.

I wished I were brave enough, fierce enough, to stand and fight, but I couldn't. Not yet. All I could do was hide in my room and make up names and draw little cities.

My city had towering buildings of light and color, some with domed tops, some with needles that tore through the sky. The roofs were flat and slanted, sprawling and thin. Some had so many windows they appeared to be constructed of glass. The sunlight caught on this glass, so unlike the dirty window in my room. The rays of light were sharp and clear, just the opposite of the dusty beams that danced lazily about in the morning. I drew a river that spilled across the landscape, a sun that didn't burn and suffocate, a paradise.

This was much, *much* worse than writing my name.

And yet, even as my gut twisted, there was a growing sense of reckless joy in my chest. I squashed it.

I had to follow protocol.

My survival depended on it.

If I managed to play along, escape unnoticed, what next? The one event every citizen in the Conurbation had to look forward to was the Acceptance ceremony; when every seventeen-year-old that year were admitted into society. The girls would wear a simple gray dress, the boys a gray suit and tie so that even then, they looked the same. It was the one ceremony that had cupcakes. The one service that had music. The one thing we were all allowed to look forward to. By then I would already be dead.

I contemplated, staring out my barred-off window.

Then, after a while, would be my graduation. From Secondary, then from Tertiary. I was reasonably intelligent, I figured I could get in a few extra years. Everyone would wear dull graduate gowns and different colored ascots; iron for one year, copper for two, bronze for three, silver for four, and gold for five years. After that, the amount of schooling didn't matter.

If I could stay for five years at Tertiary, I would be United two years later in the marriage ceremony. I would wear a traditional gray dress with a veil over my eyes, next to a stranger in a gray suit, and sign an agreement for our Unity. The event would be small, with maybe fifteen, twenty other people, the only party that involved champagne. There would be a small, white cake, perhaps decorated with delicate flowers. Roses, maybe. Or tulips. Maybe there would be tiny white pearls, studding the frosting.

More likely, there would be a simple coat of white icing. There would be enough for everyone to have a minuscule slice. One. Maybe an inch wide and three inches long. What a cause for celebration.

I would have a child with this man I'd never laid eyes on before. Or maybe I would try again and again and fail every time, would have

29

to take a forced pregnancy drug. Maybe I'd have twins. Or triplets. The maximum age between a first and second child was one year, with occasional exceptions. Possibly, I would be an exception.

What would I name the children? My children?

Wrong question. That wasn't my decision to make. My children's names would be assigned. I couldn't choose them. But if I could...

What about boys? Scorch, Jason, Bane, Fang... A little eccentric, but not terrible.

Girls would be Willow, Mal, Ember, Hazel, or maybe Lia.

Ash could go either way.

Reality would name them something more like John or Grace.

I would have two weeks with them, with this precious life I had created; two weeks to memorize their faces, their names, the color of their eyes. Two weeks to feel the softness of their skin and whisper "I love you," and hope that somehow they heard, somehow they knew.

After those two weeks, they would be gone forever.

I would leave my husband, who I'd have known for however-long-plus-nine-months-and-two-weeks, and go to my new house, my new job, my new life, except with my old memories.

I would work until I out served my usefulness. Optimistically, as Secretary, maybe as a Historian or even an Elder. Then I would be moved to live with the Seniors.

On my seventieth birthday, I would be sent to a Medical. They would ask me to lie down, to close my eyes. They would give me a shot, on my arm, and tell me to count backward from thirty. By fifteen, I would be dead, slipped into nothingness with a tiny, painless shot. I wouldn't even know whether the serum had been injected until they asked me to count. As easy as falling asleep.

Except not. I would be scared, I knew. I would be terrified. The very idea of the yawning emptiness, the sense that there might be nothing... after... was enough to make anyone feel about as significant as a grain of sand.

I have to leave, I thought. But could I? The Barrier was immense, indestructible, equipped with the highest security possible. Three hundred guards patrolled every section, each of them armed. Many notorious Rogues had tried to escape. Every single one of them was dead.

If what the Elders said was true, there was nothing out there anyways. Sand, radiation, death. Or nothing at all. But when I tried to imagine nothingness, I could only grasp a tiny piece of it before it slipped away. So that was it. Death or nothingness. Those were my choices. And this was, after all, my one home, imperfect as it was. The Elders were doing the right thing; I could perceivably start another Dark Age. And maybe I was willing to die for what was right.

This isn't what's right, a small voice inside me whispered. Killing isn't what's right.

I glanced at the time and cursed, scrambling to my feet and hauling the chest open.

Get to school now, daydream later, I scolded myself. *It can't possibly be as bad as you think it'll be.*

CHAPTER 4

School was not, in fact, as bad as I thought it would be.

It was *so* much worse.

Five men, clad in iron gray, dragged me into a gray room with a single chair.

"Sit," commanded one.

I sat.

"As you know," continued the one who had spoken first, "every citizen of the Conurbation is inspected on the day they are formally classified as an active member of society. Each member is tested and monitored for a month before they turn seventeen. Once each citizen is tested, they will endure a full year of training, learning which job position suits them best and how the society works. Each member will receive a payment of ten dollars every hour. Questions?"

"No," I said, "because, thanks to the *infallible* system, I was given *tons* of notice and was *totally* prepared for this. Thanks a lot."

There was silence.

I bit my lip.

"That kind of attitude will not be tolerated in the Conurbation. We suggest you learn fast."

I nodded, hurrying to quiet my voice so it was barely above a whisper.

"Yes sir," I apologized. "Sorry, sir."

"Very good. Now." He eyed me warily. "We are going to leave. You may do whatever you please, as long as it is in this room. Am I understood?"

"Yes, sir."

The men filed out of the room.

I sat alone. Quietly.

For several minutes I remained silent.

Then, just to hear something, *anything,* I began to tell myself a story, an idea that had been in the back of my mind for a little while, but I hadn't dared think about it. It was not pretty. It was redundant and had a childish message and I couldn't think of the right words for it, so it came out sounding all wrong. But it was my story, so I kept going.

I got about halfway through before the door burst open and guards stepped in. My heart sank; this had been a test. I had failed, miserably.

One of them said something I didn't understand, and when I didn't respond they advanced, grabbing and pushing at me.

I did the one thing I could think of.

I ran for my life.

I threw my elbow into whatever flesh I could find, sprinting as fast as my legs could carry me. I swept my foot in a full circle, knocking the guards off balance.

The moment one grabbed me I bit his arm, not letting go until the metallic tang of blood filled my mouth, warm and sticky.

I ran down winding stairwells, past perplexed teachers and bewildered students, knocking them aside, ruining their perfect lines. I darted through the cafeteria, charging past classrooms until finally, finally, I pushed through the double doors and onto the streets that drifted with orange dust.

My feet pounded the ground, kicking up sand that clogged my nose and burned my eyes. I pulled my overshirt off and wrapped it around my head, hoping to block the residue.

I wove through spidery streets, hopping the chain link fences and working my way to the outskirts of town. My gray flats kicked off and I could feel the baked sand searing my feet, little pebbles getting stuck between my toes as the coarse grains chafed my soles. The sun pounded down on my head until my hair was burning hot.

The emergency lights and sirens blared.

"Attention all Conurbation members! We have a Rogue! Repeat, we have a Rogue! Initiating lockdown sequence! Do not leave your homes! Repeat, do not leave your homes!"

Rogue was a term coined by the Elders for a Defect that dared try and escape.

I was no longer Defective and could no longer claim innocence or an easy death.

As the shock registered, my eyes began to burn, my breaths coming in rattling hitches. Warm droplets streaked down my cheeks.

I had only ever cried once, and that was when I'd overheard my Raisers speaking about me.

It was a strange feeling. I didn't remember how much it hurt; the hollowness in my chest, the aching sting in my throat, the fire behind my eyes. I didn't like showing signs of weakness. If I cried, no one would know, because crying was usually followed by taunting and sometimes assault. I'd learned long ago that if I fought someone, they'd get off without consequence and I would be punished.

And yet, as I ran, a choked sob escaped my mouth. I could not go back. I had to find a way out, maybe hide in a shop or something.

I passed the residential area, manufacturing buildings, greenhouses, and began to slow.

There was one problem.

I hadn't exactly thought this through.

Stopping in my tracks, I risked a glance backward.

The guards were right on my tail and gaining.

A surge of adrenaline rushed through my veins, and I plowed on, twice as fast as before. Typically, I wasn't anything above average when it came to athleticism. However, when my life was on the line, I could go pretty fast, plus I had a head start.

"HEY, YOU!"

I couldn't tell who the bellowing voice belonged to, I couldn't turn around to find out, I couldn't slow down. All I could do was run.

"TURN AROUND! STOP!"

I didn't.

"HEY! I AM TALKING TO YOU! STOP, OR I WILL BE FORCED TO SHOOT YOU!"

The Jurisprudents. I was so dead.

I swallowed and kept running, gasping for breath as the taste of dust and dirt smothered me, stinging my throat.

I pushed harder the buildings passed by in a blur, the booming commands fading, replaced with the pounding of my heart. My lungs began to burn. It was only when I saw a looming fence that I stopped. It was hooked forward, strung with barbed wire. I hesitated for a split second before bracing my feet on the first bar.

I strained toward the rusted metal rung that sat just out of my reach. Putting another fence between myself and my death wasn't a bad thing. The tips of my fingers hooked above at last, and I swung my foot up.

The next few bars were just as strenuous. I was wasting time. But the last pole was right there, and I seized the hooked part at the top in my fists. Muscles shaking, I pressed my feet against the metal, trying to scale a flat surface.

My skin and clothes caught on the barbed wire and tore. I grimaced, gingerly curling my toes on the rails and hoisting myself up and over. It took all my self-control to keep from screaming as my teeth dug into my lips.

A choked whimper escaped at the shredded flesh on the bottoms of my feet, at the trickles of blood swirling with dust as they ran down my ankles and dripped onto the sand. But I still slid down, mewling as sand caked my bloodied feet. Grains of it rubbed into the gashes, making me cry out.

As I bent down to brush the sand off, it encrusted the scratches in my hand and tangled itself in my hair, leaving streaks of sand and blood.

I knelt on the ground, doubling over and throwing up. Once. Twice. I gave myself until the count of five before standing and taking a few limping steps.

That was when I realized I was lost.

I leaned against a wall and looked around, falling back on my heels to keep the arches of my feet above the ground.

Here, quaint buildings, colors faded but colorful still, lined the streets.

Signs hung in their windows.

Closed Forever

It was eerie. Apartments waiting for residents that would never come home. Schools that would never teach another student. Buildings that would never be used again. Everything was different here. The roofs of each house had different styles. The walls were made of different materials. There were different colors. But the windows were boarded up. The doors were locked. Just beyond the row of buildings were greenhouses.

And now I knew where I was.

This was the Forbidden Sector.

It was the last known town from the Dark Ages. The Overseer kept it to demonstrate just how difficult history had been. Those students in their fifth year of school took a field trip to the outskirts of town to learn how treacherous it was.

If there was any chance that I would survive, my presence here just ruined it.

I sighed and wiped the sweat from my brow.

"Hey!" hissed a voice. "Over here."

A yelp escaped my mouth and I took a step back, ignoring the barking sting in my feet.

"Relax, sugar, I'm on your side." The voice had a strange, back-of-the-throat accent that I recognized but couldn't quite put a finger on, each consonant harshly enunciated. When he said 'your,' the r dropped, and 'side' was sharp and nasally.

I turned to look and saw a figure on a vehicle of sorts. A black leather seat rested in the metal, curved in the center with a sloping back. Part of it jutted over one of the tires, of which there were two.

Sleek silver exhaust pipes were mounted on each side, emitting tendrils of cool blue light. The body of the transport was the color of platinum, with handlebar grips at the front that had levers attached. A small mirror, angled so the rider could see behind himself, was positioned on the left handlebar and appeared to be adjustable.

A glass shield protected the area where I assumed one's face would be, and I noted an instrument panel, black with red lights. Black designs were spray-painted on the sides. A black plate with red lettering read *M-9*. And then I saw the passenger.

Whoever it was wore impenetrable metal armor. A titanium chest plate, mesh leggings, iron boots, aluminum gloves. A full-face helmet with tinted glass at the front that obscured his face. He was slim despite the thick armor, corded muscle visible beneath the sections of black fabric. Then he removed his helmet.

Turns out, *he* was a *she*, with dark brown skin and almond-shaped brown eyes. Half her head was shaved, the other half falling in tight curls to her chin, shiny and black. A thick scar started at the base of her jawline and disappeared under her clothes. I estimated her to be around eighteen.

"Who are you?" I asked, well aware of how I must look, haggard and bloody.

"Name's Kitty." She extended a gloved hand, eyeing the cuts on my skin. "And you'd better come with me."

CHAPTER 5

"*Look* what the *cat* dragged in," came a sarcastic drawl.

I had somehow managed to get my overshirt back on and scrub most of the blood off. I did not move as I stared at the unfamiliar, unfriendly faces around me. The room I was in was made of polished wood and metal, a refreshing change from tannish gray stone.

Metal shutters had been pulled down over the windows, but it had been some kind of living place called a "hotel" before it had been shut down. The lights were off.

Smoke filled the air, with prismatic beams swinging back and forth, reflecting off what appeared to be a mirror ball hanging from the ceiling. Blue and pink and purple with hints of green glowed all around the room. Strange, rhythmical melodies echoed through the air, loud to the point of being deafening.

People were lined up at the hotel bar, either drinking straight from the bottle or from long, slender glasses. Everyone who wasn't eating or drinking was dancing, with only about a square foot to move.

But at the sound of this voice, the talking ceased, people turning to stare at me. I could hear the silence under a layer of deafening music.

The girls wore cocktail or party dresses, miniskirts and a variety of tops, or even denim shorts, showing off more skin than fabric, and almost everything was sparkly or reflective.

They wore flashy earrings and gold bracelets and jeweled necklaces and shimmery high heels or sneakers or combat boots.

The boys wore drop-crotch pants, skinny jeans, dress pants, or long shorts, along with tank tops, shredded tee shirts, collared or button-down shirts, and a variety of embellishments.

There were chains, ear piercings, anything and everything I could imagine and more. Despite their bold accessories, they were lean and hard, with cold, fierce eyes. The unforgiving desert they had grown up in had tried to take their lives. Instead, it had robbed them of them of their humanity.

The memory of graffiti flashed before my eyes, and I somehow knew exactly who they were.

My heart stopped beating and I wanted to run but Kitty's hand was squeezing my wrist, and I couldn't move.

"Don't. Even. Think. About it," Kitty breathed, nails digging into my skin. I whimpered, trying without success to twist out of her grip and kicking her ankle out of spite once I gave up.

"Ooh," one of them mocked, "She's got some spunk, I see." This girl wore a flowing, emerald green organza blouse that was a little too sheer, revealing a low-cut black lace bra underneath, along with denim cutoffs so short that the hem almost disappeared under her shirt, flashing her long, dark legs. She had long, unnaturally straight, platinum blonde hair that had a strange sheen to it, like that wasn't her real hair color. Clasped around her neck was a delicate golden chain with a simple, teardrop emerald pendant. A freshly filled red cup was in her hand, white foam gathering at the top.

A couple of the faces I saw split into reluctant grins.

"You're one to talk," I snapped. "Your clothes could pass for underwear."

My response was met with more amusement. Everything was just a game to them, just some kind of sick joke.

"She's a Rogue. I heard the announcement. We all did. I saw her running in the FS."

"Yeah, right, cause—"

Kitty cut her off.

"Don't give me that high-and-mighty attitude just 'cause of who your brother is. This girl is twice the Rogue your friend ever was."

"My," the stranger shot back. "You're feeling confident today, aren't you?"

"Rookie," Kitty mumbled, either oblivious to the jeering crowd or accustomed to it — and I wasn't sure which was more concerning, "what's your name? Your new name, cause we ain't calling you by the one you were assigned."

I scanned the room, licking my lips. I knew better than to say "Karen." I already looked like an idiot and a coward, standing here, half-hiding behind this girl I barely knew.

"Raven," I said after a painful moment. "My name is Raven."

"'Scuse me, sorry!"

A tall, willowy girl stepped out of the shadows. She had enormous blue eyes and a massive gold bow on her head that was at least a quarter of the size of her body. She wore a canary yellow sundress that was fitted to the base of her ribcage, where it flared out and stopped at her knees, and her feet were slipped into carnation pink ballet flats. Her hair was long, loosely curled, and *very* pink.

I blinked, half wanting to touch her to make sure she was real, half wanting to cover my eyes to keep from being blinded. I had no idea how she had been so well hidden until then.

"Hullo," she beamed, extending her hand. "My name is Rose. You chose your name pretty fast. I had to take a week or so before I settled on mine."

I took it, bewildered.

"Pleasure meeting you, Rose."

She leaned in, raising her eyebrows and offering a slight smile, as if we were about to share a wonderful secret. "My favorite word is 'sunny,' my favorite things to break are windows, I like cats, witchcraft, cupcakes, music, and vandalism. And my favorite color is rainbow."

I opened my mouth and closed it. "Congratulations." *When am I ever going to use this information?*

"Rose," came a hard, quiet, yet oddly carrying voice. "Why don't you introduce everyone to our… guest." The voice was male, and the figure was in the farthest corner of the room, so covered in shadows that it was impossible to make out any distinguishing features.

"Okie dokie!" She pulled me over to the bar and took a seat, indicating I do the same. The boy next to me glanced in my direction, dull blue eyes flashing with mild irritation, before returning to the endlessly amusing task he'd been working at before, which consisted of staring at his drink.

Rose proceeded to introduce me to each person in the room, indicating everyone with a point of her finger.

Of the dozens of names I was told, I remembered four.

Jackie, a slender eighteen-ish girl with a half-shaved head like Kitty's, but honey blonde hair, and belts laden with spray paint bottles. She wore baggy, beige cargo pants and a cream-colored tank top. Tattoos curled on her neck, arms, shoulders, and chest; an intricate mosaic of patterns and images.

Obsidian, a tall twenty-three-year-old. He was a tall, gangly young man with straight black hair, black makeup, and a black-hearted scowl.

Apollo, Obsidian's three-years-younger brother and best friend, who stood a full foot shorter, with chin-length blond hair, dull blue eyes, and a black trench coat that covered every inch of his skin aside from his drawn, angular face; he was the same boy sitting next to me.

And lastly, Fas, the leader of the Murder of Crows and the figure who had requested that Rose introduce me, a nineteen-ish young man with both sides of his head shaved, leaving a chin-length strip of hair in the middle, combed to the side. The roots and tips of his hair were black, and the rest of it was dyed the color of bluebird feathers, varying paler shades mixed in. He had a tight tank top, white combat boots, well-toned muscles, and tan skin. His glowing, serpentine eyes settled on me. And stayed there. My heart skipped a beat, even as my face remained a blank mask.

"Everyone, this is Raven. Raven, this is everyone," Rose concluded.

I didn't really know what to do, so I just rocked back on my heels and nodded, pressing my lips together.

"Remember everyone?" Rose asked as the people before me drifted back to their former places, conversation beginning to flow throughout the room again.

I let out a long breath of air and grinned. "Sure."

"It's okay," she assured me. "I forgot their names too."

Jackie shifted closer to the girl Kitty had called high-and-mighty, murmuring something that made the girl smile and look away, tucking a lock of long hair behind her ear.

CHAPTER 6

"Jackie— darling— is it *necessary* to take the rookie?" Obsidian whined, wrinkling his nose as he slid a knife from his boot. I couldn't figure out what about him annoyed me so much— maybe he was just an annoying person.

I had no idea how Rose had talked me into this, but here I was, turning a small, sharp stone over in my hands. I would collect more when it was time.

What would breaking windows sound like?

"Today probably isn't the best day," Apollo agreed, lifting the wine glass to his lips. His fingers tapped the side of it, compulsive, like a spasm. "Not that anyone cares or anything." Jackie's response and his retort were lost on me; I didn't understand half of what anyone was saying as it was.

"So, aren't you, like, the most wanted faces in all the Conurbation?" I put in, cutting Apollo off and earning myself a cold stare. "Shouldn't you be a little more careful?"

"If *anyone* here was careful, we'd all be dead." Apollo's expression was one of cruel amusement as he knocked another drink back. "You'd be dead, too, actually."

I bit the inside of my cheek and elected not to reply.

We rode in a sleek black car, the headlights off, the inside lights off.

Silent. I had never been in a car before, never seen one. The inside had three rows: two seats, two seats, three seats.

I rode in the back, crammed between two girls called Crystal and Dove. Jackie drove, and Rose sat next to her, with Obsidian and Apollo sitting side by side, hands clasped in a casual, comforting way, a way that I supposed was brotherly, mostly because I had no idea what brotherly looked like.

My feet and hands were bound in white gauze, slathered in cleansing and healing ointment. The wounds had already been infected when I arrived, and the city's Medical had mercifully knocked me out before cleaning me up. Rose had changed into a black miniskirt, black collared silk organza blouse, black mesh leggings, and black sneakers. She had replaced her huge gold bow with a huge black one. No matter how dark her outfit, though, she had no hope of disguising that *hair.*

There was a feature that cooled the inside of the car, and another that heated it. We could roll the windows up and down, see just how fast we were going, how much gas we had left, and there were cupholders. *Cupholders.*

To a girl who had spent almost seventeen years living in monotony, this was absolute magic.

Rose turned the sound on.

There was a boy singing, with a beautiful voice and beautiful words.

"And yes, Obsidian—" Jackie mocked, turning down the music before I could make out more, "darling— we do have to bring her. She's just gotten here; don't you think she'll want to get a taste of what it feels like to get even?"

"Maybe," Apollo said. "But no one really cares what she wants, right?"

I *wanted* to say something, to tell him off. Nothing came to mind, though, so I just glared at the back of his head.

He met my eyes in the rearview and offered a humorless grin.

Maybe I'd be as tired as he was if it weren't for the surges of adrenaline that ripped through my blood, or the butterflies in my stomach, or my sudden and inexplicable thirst for revenge. *Revenge is bad,* I thought, the voice in my head a sarcastic imitation of my teacher's voice.

"Vengeance was the nature of our ancestors," she had said. *"But we are no longer so primitive."*

If this was humanity's idea of advanced, I was terrified of learning what primitive looked like.

I had seen that cruelty in the horrible satisfaction in the eyes of the guards as they attacked me, knowing that finally, finally, they had something to tear apart.

Something to destroy.

The Elders said that no individual was placed below the rest.

That wasn't true.

"Apollo," Obsidian hissed. "Apollo!"

He reached over and shook his brother's shoulder. Apollo stirred.

"Mmmh," he complained, rubbing his eyes.

"Sweetheart, how much wine did you have?" Obsidian asked, voice saccharine in a way that didn't quite match the sharp suspicion in his gaze.

Apollo's lips twitched downward, and he pushed his hair out of his eyes. He leveled a flat stare at his brother, but other than that, there was no reply.

Obsidian fixed him with an angry glare. This got a bit more of a response; Apollo pushed himself forward, bracing one hand on the headrest in front of him.

"Honestly." He rolled his eyes, dragging out the *h* in *honestly*, and opened the window, leaning out and twisting around to look behind us. His gloved hands tensed on the car door. "Get down," he said, rather calmly, as he plopped back into his seat.

"What?" Obsidian stared at him.

"Get," Apollo repeated. "Down. Now. Everyone."

Obsidian's mouth opened and closed a couple times.

"Darling, you're not making any sense—" His voice was pleading.

"Come on!" Apollo hissed. "Seriously? Are you going to move, or should I—"

There was an earsplitting *crack* as something small and round careened through the window.

Apollo pulled out a sleek metal weapon, black with a barrel in front and a trigger near the handle. He twisted and fired, explosive noise hammering my ears.

Another bullet shot through the window.

"Faster!" Crystal shrieked.

The tires squealed on the pavement as Jackie slammed her foot on the gas pedal.

We sped down roads and alleyways, maneuvering through the maze of streets.

When I looked out the window, I saw darkness.

The only thing scarier than being attacked was not being able to see your attacker.

They didn't have a car. That was something, wasn't it? I tried to focus on that. They did not have a car, they did not have a car, they did not have a car—

A white, battered van pulled up behind us.

"Holy hell," I whispered. "They have a car."

A fist crashed through the windshield of their car, followed by a machine gun. Someone pulled the trigger.

I startled and let loose a stream of curses I'd forgotten I actually knew.

Some instinct kicked in and I ducked, pulling the two other girls down with me before I got hurt worse than I already was, before I got a bullet hole in addition to the cuts on my back from the glass.

Jackie wasn't so lucky.

I saw the second bullet fly towards her, saw her eyes widen, saw it hit her shoulder and lodge itself there. Bright red blood gushed from the wound, surrounding the metallic shape.

She made a surprised noise, swerving to one side.

"Jackie!" Rose cried, seizing her friend's wrist. "Don't pass out, don't pass out, don't pass out—"

"Please stop," Jackie whispered. She reached one hand back and curled her fingers on her shoulder, flinching back when she brushed the wound. "Ow," she added, closing her eyes.

"I CAN'T TAKE THE WHEEL FROM HALFWAY ACROSS THE CAR!" Rose screeched. There was no response.

"Ugh," Apollo groaned, unsnapping his seatbelt. "I love dying, don't you, Rose?" He twisted around to shoot over my head again and laughed when I threw my hands up over my face.

Rose stretched out and managed to grab the wheel by her fingertips. "No. That's *your* job. And, just so we're clear—"

She didn't get to finish her sentence, due to an unfortunate thing called the Barrier, the wall that surrounded the Conurbation.

I could hear the metal buckling, the tinkling of glass as the window broke. Jackie came to with a gasp, hitting the breaks without even trying to pull the glass shards from her skin. The tires shrieked in protest as the car tipped over with a groan. The roof caved so fast, I didn't have time to scream. Warm liquid trickled down the side of my head and into my mouth, sticky and metallic.

For a moment, there was silence. I got up first, unbuckling my seatbelt and edging sideways down to the doors.

"Mind telling me what you're doing, sweetie?" Obsidian moaned, rubbing his already-bruised forehead.

"Are you kidding me?" I lashed. "We just spent the night chased around by a bunch of psychopaths! Do you really think I'm going to sit here and wait for them to finish the job? Jackie needs to get to the infirmary, like, right now."

The door slid open and I jumped out, bending my knees as my feet hit the pavement. My head swung from side to side as I searched for any possible enemies.

"There's no one out here," I called.

One by one, each of the others in the car hopped out.

Jackie's head leaned against Rose's shoulder, small trails of blood tracing down her skin.

"Where are the Normal who attacked us?" Dove asked.

"We killed them," Apollo said. "Or, rather, I did, seeing as no one else was sane enough to bring a gun..."

His eyes widened.

I blinked, and when my eyes opened again, there was a hole in his stomach. Obsidian's hand flew to his mouth.

Seemingly undaunted, Apollo inspected the bleeding bullet hole in his abdomen with a sort of dull interest in his eyes.

"Thought they'd suspect something," he muttered.

His eyes rolled up into the back of his head and he passed out on the sidewalk.

I grimaced.

"Ouch."

Obsidian stared at the limp figure of his younger brother lying on the ground. Expressionless, he leaned down and pulled the gun from Apollo's belt.

Spinning on his heel, Obsidian shot the last bullet into darkness.

I heard a cry, then silence.

CHAPTER 7

Fas stood before us, eyes smoldering.

I leaned on a curved white metal shelf, stacked with holo cards and file folders. The lamps cast a warm, yellowish light across the room, clashing with the utter darkness outside.

"And the soldiers," he started, with that strange, underlying hiss that sent chills down my back. "They had guns. And cars. Which they are not supposed to have."

Crystal nodded.

"And now two of our Crows are in the infirmary."

"Yeah," I replied, tugging the bandage tighter around my leg and watching red splotches spread across the gauze. "Sounds about right, except you forgot about our car tipping over."

"And they managed to hit Jackie," he said. "And Apollo, who had a gun."

"Yup."

Fas leaned against the wall, rubbing his mohawk.

"They're up to something."

"No," I snapped. "Really?"

Ignoring my sarcasm, Fas continued, "Their behaviors over the past month have been... concerning." He ran his tongue over his teeth in a not-quite-natural way.

"You mean more concerning than *your* behavior?" I asked. "Because I have to disagree with you there, sir."

This time my remark earned me a cold glare. "More cameras, harsher punishments. You know how it works." His eyes darted around, landing on me and staying there.

Something about his gaze was inhuman, and I suppressed a shudder. Apparently satisfied with my discomfort, Fas stood.

"Our scouts will continue to look into this matter." He tilted his head. "Go to bed or get yourselves cleaned up in the infirmary. I don't care which."

Okay then.

Rose led me down a dark, winding hallway. Doors lined each side, with evenly spaced, rectangular lights hanging from the ceiling. The floor was covered in a patterned, black and white carpet, and both Rose and I padded barefoot down the hall.

"You're my roommate!" she gushed. "Isn't that the greatest? Dove and Crystal and Jackie are gonna be with us too! So cool, right?"

I nodded, preoccupied as the scene played over in my head.

I had never once seen anyone kill someone else in my entire life.

Of course, I knew that Defects were killed, Rogues suffered longer. But until now, that had all been a theory, a vague threat. And of course, I knew that, had the others not defended themselves, we'd all be worse than dead. But I'd never thought I would have to witness someone's death.

Obsidian had picked up the gun with so little emotion, like he knew what would happen next. He hadn't even hesitated.

The look on his face was pure vengeance.

And I felt nothing more than a shaking numbness. I was startled but no more.

"Raven!"

I glanced back to see Rose waiting by an iron door about ten feet behind where I stood.

"Oops," I said, squashing the sheepishness in my voice. "Sorry."

"It's all right," Rose offered. "I'm sure you must feel terrible."

"I wish I could say I did," I admitted. "But I can't because that would be lying."

Rose shrugged and pushed open the door.

The room was made of faded oak planks, two walls of it stacked in a horizontal position. Two floor-to-ceiling windows took up the other walls, separated by thin strips of white. Two beds were pushed against the wood, separated by a sleek black nightstand. The mattresses were the same ones in the Conurbation, but they were doubled up and re-stuffed, with a new cover on them that looked smooth and soft.

The comforters were puffy and cool to the touch, the pillows plumped and luxurious. Pendant lamps hung from the ceiling, silk organza curtains hanging on either side of the window, the bed frames weathered and rough in a cozy, comfortable way. A granite area rug rested on the hardwood floors. And there was a Recamier couch against the window with four throw pillows on it, along with black porcelain vases on either side. The visible cushion was covered in fancy letters I could barely read.

I didn't register any of it. All I could see was what was out the window.

Rolling, aquamarine waves, sparkling like glass in the daylight. An azure sky scattered with puffy white clouds. Topaz, sapphire, and hints of emerald glistened in the sun. Amber glints sparked beneath them. They slammed and caressed the fine sand, gray and tan and soft. Right where earth met water, a mix of colorful pebbles tossed and turned on the sand. I could hear the faint roar and hiss as it dragged out and into itself and I could smell the salt in the air and wind. It was beautiful, it was fearsome, it was spellbinding and entrancing.

I whirled; eyes wide.

"What is it?" I breathed. "How is it there?" I raced to the window and pressed my hands against it, wondering if there was anything I could ever love more.

"It's not," Rose giggled. "We're in the desert. It's a hologram. Tracks the progress of the sun, unless you turn that off."

"What is it?" I demanded.

"The ocean. It's not there."

"I *love* it. Is that sand?"

"Yes, much better than the red stuff outside, isn't it?"

"Yeah." I traced my finger down the glass.

"Here," Rose said. "You can sleep on the bed next to mine! It's closest to the window. I assume you want to tour the rest of the place another time."

"Thanks," I replied, my mind still on the ocean. "Yeah."

I wondered what happened to compassion as I strode to the bathroom to change, because at least six fellow human beings had died, and I didn't care. At least I could blame my upbringing for that.

The sleep clothes were silky and a bluish pink color that I liked, the shorts hemmed with scalloped lace. The top had thin straps, the same lace hemming, and a sweetheart neckline. My still-bare feet curled on the textured beige tile on the floor.

I wished I would cry; I wanted to scream and pummel the mattress and curl up into a little ball and act like a bawling Fledgling. But I didn't, because this was life, and these things happened. I should have been guilty, at least pensive, but no. For every seventeen-year-old who died believing there was something wrong with them, I was remorseless. For every ten-year-old who ran away because no one was there for them. For every life taken, for every abandoned infant, I. Was. Glad. Those men deserved a slower death.

I couldn't cry, and I knew it. Because I didn't care.

I stood from the bed and touched the activation holo lightly, spinning the dial back. The scene faded, revealing the city outside.

Just like it always was, as though nothing had changed.

As I turned away, an explosion thundered in the distance, a column of smoke shooting up from the ground and curling into itself. I forced my gaze away and slid the holo back into place.

My horrible fascination with the destruction of carefully constructed buildings was unsettling and nothing more. I watched the glittering, pristine sea and listened to the sound of Dove and Crystal enter without a sound.

Now that Rose had turned the switch off, the water was a deep, midnight blue, mirroring the night sky above. The moon hung a little above the horizon, painting a silver strip down the center of the ocean that was broken up by glittering waves. A pathway to heaven, to paradise, to someplace better. The rocks farther down the beach jutted out like shards of glistening onyx. Every once in a while, a wave would slam into these rocks, causing a spray of water to spring into the air. Eventually, the ocean lulled me to sleep.

I was standing in a bathroom. It was unlike the cold, clean bathrooms of the Conurbation, and also unlike the luxurious bathrooms in my new home. The tile was cracked and grimy, words scrawled on the wall. I did not know their meaning.

A filthy, cream-colored toilet was next to me, the lid chipped in several places. A single lightbulb guttered above me, occasionally sending sparks into the air. The mirror was shattered, pieces of glass strewn across the floor, cutting my bare feet. In the remaining fragments, I saw my reflection, but... not.

A young woman with a complexion that closely resembled mine beamed at me from my reflection. Her jet-black hair was much longer, hanging around her waist in a straight curtain. Her eyes were almond-shaped and blue, undertones of purple sparkling where the light hit.

Her ears were more pointed than mine, locks of hair tucked behind one. But she looked, other than that, almost exactly like me.

And that's when I knew: somehow, it was my mother staring back at me.

She reached out as though to touch me, before pulling back.

"Look at you," she breathed. "Look how much you've grown. Look how beautiful you are."

"Mother—" I began, voice breaking.

"Wake up," came the sibilate voice, jolting me out of sleep. It was dark, male, and it had a crisp, cultured edge. I jumped and kicked out before my eyes were even open, catching whoever it was in the stomach. He gave a low grunt, but he was as solid as a rock, impossible to harm.

"Who are you?" I demanded, yanking the covers up to my collarbone. "Why are you *in* here?"

"I've come," he said, and I could sense him approaching, "to try and figure you out."

"Why."

"Do I need a reason?"

"Yes, you arrogant—"

The lights flicked on.

Now I could make out his features. His inky black hair was neatly combed to the side, complementing the strong set of his jaw.

Rose didn't stir as he frowned at me, his eyes like molten gold. He was slender yet muscular, his skin dark enough that his straight, white teeth seemed to glow.

He had a simple gold chain resting at his throat, and he was dressed in darkly colored formal attire.

There was a light stubble on his cheeks, as though he'd forgotten to shave, but other than that his skin was perfect. There was something eerily calm about him, along with a sophisticated air. Elegant brutality.

I opened my mouth, but he silenced me with a single glance.

Whatever you're about to say, his gaze suggested, *save it for someone who cares.*

His flat expression made it hard to tell, but I was pretty sure he was smirking. My glare could've knocked him over.

66

He offered me his hand.

"Walk with me," he suggested.

On the one hand, I didn't trust random strangers who showed up in my bedroom. On the other hand, *I didn't trust random strangers who showed up in my bedroom*. But on the third hand...

I took his hand and stood.

CHAPTER 8

The hallways were dark; I had no idea where we were.

"Where are we going?" I asked.

"It would be better if you didn't talk for now. People are sleeping." His words were kind enough, but his tone was icy; I did as I was told.

After some time, I saw a dim light, sliding through the cracks of a set of double doors. He pushed one open and held it for me so I could go inside ahead of him, and I found that the hallway opened into an enormous room.

The walls were a deep, dark red, with cream curtains and gold accents. The floor was a polished, rich brown, although it was scuffed from having not been cleaned for a long time. Ornate pillars lined the wall, painted with what might have been real gold, but that wasn't the best part.

In the middle of the room, hanging from the vaulted ceilings, was a light fixture of some kind, made up of thousands of shards of glass cut into tiny prisms, scattering the light so it danced in rainbows across the room. They hung in tiers, with the centermost tier consisting of a single teardrop pendant.

All of it was beautiful, in a sad, washed-out way. A ghost, that's what this was. The spirit of some long-ago time when luxury wasn't some wicked overindulgence, it was a privilege.

It took me a moment to realize that he was watching me, his golden eyes burning a hole in my shoulders.

It took me another moment to regain the ability to breathe and yet another to realize I was gaping.

He tilted his head at me, a catlike curiosity in his eyes.

"Speechless," he said drily. "That's certainly new." My smile dropped, and I turned my hand back and forth, so the mini rainbows glowed on my fingers like multicolored rings.

"It's beautiful," I admitted, "but why are we in here?"

He didn't answer for a few seconds.

"Tell me about yourself, Raven," he said at last.

"That's not an answer."

He ignored this.

"What made you Defective?" he asked.

"Your guess is as good as mine."

"That's not an answer," he mocked. "You have to know. It's not as though you're an Aberration or anything." He widened his eyes at me, waiting for my response, seeing how I would react.

"What's an Aberration? Wait, hold on. What's your *name?*"

"You may call me any name you like."

"I can think of a few good ones," I snapped, taking a step back to the intricate double doors.

"Just answer my question." He seemed baffled by me, yet intrigued, something feline in his poise.

"Lots of things," I said. "I fought people and thought the wrong thoughts; for all you know I'm a cold-blooded murderer."

He twisted to get a better look at me, taking in every detail of my face, maybe committing it to memory.

"What's your favorite color?" he asked, sounding indifferent.

"I don't know what that means."

"The term is self-explanatory."

This stopped me for a minute. Favorite color. I could have one of those now? Which color was my favorite? I had seen four colors so far that I recognized: red, green, yellow, blue. Of course, I had seen several others that I didn't know. I knew which one I liked best, but I was never taught the color's name.

"What's this color?" I asked, fingering the fabric of my sleepwear. It was the right color, except with too much red.

He glanced at it, then back at me.

"Purple," he said. "There are different shades and tones–"

"That," I interrupted him. "But with more blue."

"Purple." He sounded amused, fixing me with his unsettling gold eyes. He caught himself and looked down again.

Maybe this was a bad idea. Perhaps I should've just stayed in bed. Or kicked him harder. Probably I should just go back now and not come back...

He met my eyes in a way that told me he was smiling, just without his mouth. A truce. I smiled back.

"You should go," he said, voice uncharacteristically gentle. "It's getting late."

When I woke up the next morning, I thought maybe it was a dream. Even so, I scanned the crowds to see if I could find him. He was nowhere.

The flat screen televisions in the hotel lobby activated with a soft noise. A broadcast appeared, causing many to stop and watch.

This was one of their scare tactics, I realized— they'd hack the school holograms, play a creepy video, and leave.

There, on the screen, was a scene of chaos. The bomb fell, crashing into the roof of the substantial concrete building, and detonated. The windows exploded outwards, the frame shattering. The top three floors collapsed into the lower levels, and a field of dust burst out, stirring up the desert sand.

Fas's face appeared, and he started talking, something about a countrywide power outage. But I wasn't listening.

Rose took me on a tour around the Forbidden Sector, showing me how to use their currency, called capitals, which were small, rectangular aluminum, silver, and silicon bars which ranged in value based on the metal's size and purity.

She took me into a place with a wide selection of clothing items, the kinds of clothes I had seen at that first party. The room had a variety of reflective panels lining either side, along with small doors made of the same glass-like material. Those led to places where you could try on the clothes, even if they weren't yours yet. It wasn't illegal, though, according to Rose. And if it were, it wouldn't really matter, considering there were more significant problems at hand.

On the ceiling was a spiked metal light fixture, again made of the "mirrors" on the walls. It pulsed softly with golden light, casting fragments of it across the marble floor. Round white chairs sat across from one another, a black table between them.

"There are multiple stores like this one?" I asked the owner, who smiled, playing with his ear piercing.

"That's how this system works," he explained. "It takes some getting used to, but it's a good way of going about things. The stores compete, and the ones without enough funding don't survive. But then you can choose certain stores based on your own style."

I pulled back, eyes widening slightly. "Really?"

He nodded, grin broadening at the look on my face before Rose dragged me off.

Racks of clothing sat in neat rows in the back. I lifted a white cotton shirt with wide slashes across the back and sides, the collar having been ripped off.

"Someone was very offended at the existence of this garment," I observed, to Rose's amusement.

"No," she said with a smile. "People wear that."

I stared at her. "With *what*?"

"Never mind," she insisted, waving her hands. "We're here to buy you stuff!"

She selected a loose white shirt, denim shorts, black leggings made of beautiful, lace thorn patterns, and red "sneakers" for me.

They were made of a thick meshy material, tied up in strings. The soles were rubber, built for comfort rather than practicality.

There was a cap, with a stiff visor designed to keep the sun from my eyes. A baseball hat.

"What's baseball?" I'd asked.

"You know what? Never mind."

I also chose a pair of tinted pieces of glass, framed with gold wire.

"Pilot glasses," Rose explained. "They're a type of sunglasses." Sunglasses were not, in fact, pieces of the sun trapped inside shards of glass, as I had thought. They would shield my eyes from harmful UV rays.

The other two outfits I found to my liking had a similar style. A white, spaghetti-strapped tank top with a low-cut neckline that I gaped at for a moment before getting over myself. *Try something new,* I thought, enjoying the flipping sensation in my stomach. *Better gawked at than dead.* Although I got the feeling I would blend in just fine.

Black jeans, black leather wedge boots, a black leather satchel with gold zippers and clasps.

My third decision was on a pair of torn up, faded denim shorts, high to the point of scandalizing. The oversized, loose gray shirt colorfully declared its hatred of the Conurbation, so I grabbed that as well. A wide range of leather bracelets along with scuffed-up black combat boots completed the look. I hoped I didn't look like a bumbling idiot. Rose told me that I could interchange various garments to make different outfits.

"This is much more exciting than my regular routines," I admitted as Rose insisted on paying.

"Well duh." She poked my nose. "That's the point, silly!"

I pushed open the glass doors – bulletproofed – and continued to stroll down the black stone corridor. I had tried to go outside once, and the blonde girl had almost killed me.

"We don't go outside!" she'd hissed. "*People* are outside! And their cameras! Gods above, Rookie, I didn't think you were that stupid!"

I rolled my eyes at the memory, freezing in front of yet another brand-new building. They seemed to pop up overnight, and the new spaces sent chills down my back for a few days after their construction. This one was like most of the others, stout and glass with a metal frame. I hadn't been through the concealed hallway that lead inside it yet, but it was supposed to be an educational center. Perhaps this was Fas's plan– to gradually take up more and more of the country we hid in the corner of.

I paused near a poster of a gorgeous woman with rippling black hair. Her head was tilted to the side and rivers of stars and galaxies flowed like tears from under her heavily lidded eyes, lined with silver. Her full lips were painted a soft purple.

"Oh, that." Rose grinned, following my gaze. "Galaxy couture. It's very popular right now; there's blush, eyeshadow, lipstick. I really like the lipstick. Let's get some later!"

I laughed and shook my head.

Rose jumped and waved at two girls with odd makeup. "That's Mal and Lilianna!" As they drew nearer, I saw that the one called Mal had dewy metallic skin with iridescent pinks and greens and grays.

And Lilianna...

Her head was shaved bald, and she wore gray sweatpants and a white tank top. But her skin was deathly pale, dark makeup surrounding her eyes and nose. White teeth were visible where her mouth should have been, stretching the length of her jaw, which was shaded in detail.

A skull, I realized, that's what this was. Her throat was black with ivory vertebrae drawn down to her chest, where I could see her sternum, ribs, and clavicles. Her shoulders down bared her arm and hand bones, the rest black. Like an X-ray screen. She waved a grotesquely detailed hand as she passed, displaying every bone in her fingers.

"And this," she chirped, tugging me inside, "is called a café. You can buy coffee, or tea, or chips, or cookies, or-"

"What are cookies?" I asked.

She stopped, staring at me.

"You don't know what a cookie is?" she shrilled. "That is cruel and unusual *punishment!* I mean, I know the Stringers are horrible, but that is just a crime against *humanity!* Come on, come on, come *on!*"

The aromas hit me almost a little too hard. Thick, creamy, silky smooth, almost like the smell of chocolate, which I'd been introduced to earlier that day, but sharper. The walls were stacked with ply boards and polished wood, with a big bowl filled with greenish water and lily pads sitting in the center.

Rose dragged me over to the granite counter, where a girl (wasn't her name Aquila or something? Aquola? Aqu-something. It was Aqu-something) was arranging cups and straws and marking inventory in a notebook. A chalkboard behind her had been inscribed with neat lettering.

~: ~

Today's Specials

Chai Tea

Passionfruit Tea

Cream Espresso

Cafe Au Lait

~· ~

"Hello," the young woman paused, finishing the note she was taking down before looking up to smile. "How may I help you?"

"I'll take the Cafe Au Lait," Rose offered. She glanced at me. "And my friend will take the sweetened Passionfruit."

I tapped her shoulder. "What's that?"

"Wait and see," Rose said.

"Okay," the girl behind the counter said, tapping on her keyboard. "That'll be... Ah, seven capitals. Is that acceptable?"

"Of course," Rose sang, dropping seven aluminum pieces on the counter.

Light from the windows glanced off each piece, making them glow a brilliant silver.

The young lady swept them up, counting them under her breath, before placing them carefully in a metal container.

Rose dismissed all my questions with a flippant "I'll explain later" and took me back out into the hallway.

CHAPTER 9

The club was a lot like the hotel room I had arrived in. It was loud, and crowded, and there was a bar, a big glittery ball, smoke, and laser lights swinging back and forth. Loud noise blared through speakers, a steady pulse with rhythms and voices weaving through it, creating a frenzied beat with people jumping up and down to it. A glowing white pool with railings dipping into the water. Honeycomb lights hung from the ceiling. Bowl-shaped rubber seats sat in circles on raised platforms in the water. Balconies shoved out from the second level. Golden jugs rested at random, bringing out the soft purple glow that emanated from the lights and pool.

A girl tumbled off one of the balconies, before catching herself by the tips of her fingers and swinging herself back up with a dramatic flourish. Her friends above laughed for a minute before helping her over the rail. It was the girl from earlier, the one with the too-sheer green shirt.

"Well, *someone's* drunk," Dove commented, pulling her whitish-blue hair out of her eyes. She paused and glanced around. "Where's Crystal? I see Obsidian, but not Apollo, and—"

Rose scoffed.

"He. Is. So. *Annoying*," she gritted. "Almost as annoying as the Normals."

Normals. Stringers. These were the words I heard thrown around to describe the Conurbation citizens. I wasn't sure how to react to these names, but I supposed *Citizens of the Conurbation* was a little too long-winded.

"And *you're* the reason three new rules were added," Dove chimed, not even slowing down as she danced.

"Yeah, well," Rose smirked. "You know. Stuff happens."

"What do you mean?" I asked.

"I threw a training knife at him. He still has the scar."

"The one on his face?"

"No. That one's always been there. *I'm* talking about the one on his hand, when he tried to deflect it."

I blinked.

"I threw the knife at him," Rose continued, "and he put his hands up to protect his face. The knife went straight through."

I could feel the blood draining from my face.

"Straight–" I stammered, "straight through? His *hand?*"

"Straight through," Rose agreed.

Dove burst out cackling at the look on my face and dragged Rose back to the dance floor.

Fas came up next to me and watched them for a moment before turning. A rare, crooked smile was on his face, like he was genuinely enjoying himself.

"Wanna dance?" he asked, grin splitting wider with feline delight as he saw my expression.

"Wow," I said. "You're drunk, aren't you?"

"Maybe." He shifted his cup, and I saw a glowing gold liquid slosh around inside.

"What's that?" I inquired, trying to grab it for a better look. Fas held it out of my reach, amusement gleaming in his eyes.

"Not for you," he said over the music, tipping the rest of it into his mouth.

"Dance?" he offered again, and this time, I allowed him to lead me onto the floor.

He pulled me closer, folding my hands into his and keeping his grasp a respectful distance away from my waist and legs. His fingers were warm, hot, even, matching the heated temperature of the room. But even as I danced with him, my mind was elsewhere, in another, much quieter room.

"Who even plans these parties?" I asked, shouting a little so he could hear me over the music.

"Who do you think?" he murmured, somehow making his voice carry over the chaos. He cast a glance to the balcony, where the blonde girl had climbed back up and was smiling sheepishly at her friends. She caught his gaze and grinned broadly, lifting a cup. Then her grasp slipped, and she dropped her drink, glowing gold liquid splashing on everyone. She lifted her head to meet Fas's eyes, hand flying to her mouth. The corner of his lip tugged down.

"Who's that?" I asked.

"She's my sister," Fas replied absently, still looking at her. His hair gleamed a dull aquamarine in the neon light.

"You don't look related at all."

"I dyed my hair. She bleached it."

"Oh," I said, only half understanding.

Fas held my hands tighter and tore his gaze away from the girl, pulling me into a soothing rhythm.

Four hours and a pair of aching legs later, I collapsed into bed, having finally forgotten about that strange boy.

But he came back that night.

He seemed a little unsteady, and his eyes were tired, but he was waiting nonetheless.

Another silent smile made just for me, another hand hovering in the air, an offer, a request.

That night we danced in the ballroom, even though my legs hurt, even though I was exhausted. Slow, soft, hopeful sounds in the background that he explained to me as music, not the kind that blasted at all the parties. I loved it. Even if he stumbled twice.

"Were you at the party tonight?"

He smiled, gold eyes glinting. "Everyone was at the party tonight."

"I didn't see you."

An odd look crossed his face.

"*I* saw you," he told me.

I dismissed the suspicion building in my chest and let him sweep me away.

All I could think of the following morning was the music, his arms around me, the ballroom, no one left in the world but me and the beautiful boy of shadows.

Rose dragged me to yet another bookstore and bought book in a series about something I didn't understand. Her voice had gotten all breathy and fast when she was explaining it and I couldn't hear a word she said. But when she calmed down, she convinced me to buy the holo card for one with lots of pretty colors and fancy lettering on the cover.

The walls were rounded and stacked with holo cards, each glowing with a colored light. The lights were organized by genre, and there would be tints or shades of the color based on the difficulty of the book. The ceiling was made from reflective metal, giving the illusion of a much larger room. Small tables with lamps in the middle of each one lined the keyhole-shaped chamber. Rose explained that there used to be plain white paper, but whatever was left had to be saved for a matter of utmost importance. I thought of the holograms of old books, with smooth white pages and neat type, paper that was at everyone's disposal.

Why would the Conurbation take that away?

No matter what anyone thought, the Forbidden Sector was the closest thing to paradise I had ever seen.

After the bookstore Rose (and, by extension, me) went to something called a "salon." It was a place where they styled our hair, changed the way it looked, its shape, its color. Rose added a darker pink to the ends of her hair, giving it a cool fading effect. She picked up a pack of green and gold dye for Jackie to add streaks to her hair. I washed the dull brown color out, revealing the stark black my hair really was. I bleached the ends before coloring them a royal purple.

The dye job wasn't free, so there was a counter for paying at the front of the shop, topped with black-and-white granite.

Fas was there, arguing with the cashier.

"Excuse me," Rose said, holding the unpaid dye.

"You can wait," Fas snarled. He looked about as tired as I felt.

"Oh, hey Fas," I snapped. "Forgot to ask you. How's the hangover?"

Fas blinked, face going blank.

"I don't *get* hangovers," he informed me, still with that unsettling nothingness in his expression.

"You aren't intimidating," I flicked my hair over my shoulder. "Come on, it'll take, like, *two seconds.* At most."

He raised an eyebrow but moved so Rose could check out.

"Finally," Rose said as we left, hurrying down the dark hallway and glancing out a window at the sun. "We don't have much time left today."

She bought a tattoo catalog holo chip to bring Jackie for her recovery. I didn't know why Jackie needed *more*, but supposedly she enjoyed getting them. She already had more tattoos than I could count, but among them, I noticed a fire bird, a skull, a cat's eye, an arrow, an armband, and some kind of geometric sun-and-moon. That was just what I could make out among the crowded thorns and vines.

When I asked if it hurt to get them, Rose only shrugged and said she'd never gotten one, so she didn't know.

I'd bunched my lips to the side, considering, before sitting in one of the black leather chairs and asking for a tattoo. I'd almost changed my mind when I saw the needle, but I went with the one that caught my eye: a large creature of scales and claws and huge wings and a whip-like tail. It coiled around my arm near my shoulder, inked in black.

An hour and four shopping trips later my skin was still sore.

When I drifted off that night, the first thing I thought of was that strange boy, who I'd started calling Shadow in my head. Seemed appropriate, considering his nightly tendencies.

"Change," ordered the smooth, cold male voice that shook me from sleep. A moment later, a bundle of fabric landed in my lap.

My eyes cracked open enough for me to see that he was smiling. I rolled over and mumbled something obscene.

"Come on," he coaxed.

"Why should I change into that?" I demanded, my voice muffled by the pillow. "My clothes are practical enough."

"You should wear it," Shadow said, "because I want to dance with you, and because I think it'll look nice."

"Of *course*, your majesty." This was an insult in the book I'd gotten; the main character used it on someone almost as self-entitled as the boy standing over me now. Even so, I opened my eyes again to look at the dress he'd tossed onto my bed. The gown itself was simple; white fabric, a sweetheart cut, flowing to ankle length. The beauty lay in the bodice, which was draped with strands of rich purple jewels and fine gold chains that wreathed and coiled down my waist and thighs.

I dragged my gaze from the dress and looked at the amused grin on Shadow's face.

"It looks very heavy," I murmured. His smile faltered a little, a bit of disappointment slipping through. Not at me, but more at himself for not picking a gown I liked.

I propped myself up on my elbows.

"Remind me why you're in here right now?" I grumbled.

"I–"

"No," I cut him off. "I mean, why wait until nighttime to talk to me?"

"I have… things to do during the day," he sighed, rubbing his forehead.

"What kind of things?" I asked, easing into a sitting position.

"So many questions," he purred. "Is this you avoiding the dress?"

"No, I'm just curious." I pushed off the bed and grabbed the gown, heading to the bathroom to change, but not before sticking my tongue out over my shoulder at him.

I let him style my hair into a loose bun, let him lead me, barefoot, down the hall and shush me when I laughed. I let him take me into that room, let him hold me by the waist and tell me to put my feet on his. Now I was almost at eye level with him, my toes curling on the leather of his boots. I looked over his shoulder as I clasped my hands behind his neck, watching the light from the chandelier play on the wood panels.

The music was pure and melodic, pulsing in rhythm with Shadow's steps.

I lost track of time, twirling in that empty room, learning the movements to each dance, some deep and soulful, others bright and merry. My dress billowed around me when I jumped or twisted, or when he lifted me above his head.

"What's this?" Shadow asked, stopping to move my sleeve up and touching my bandage. I shivered, feeling how cold he was through the fabric. The tattoo was still sore.

I shrugged and fingered the jewels on the bodice.

"A tattoo. No big deal."

"Did you get it today?"

"Yeah, I guess."

"For a Rookie, you certainly do quite a bit during the day."

"Speaking of which, do you *ever* sleep?" I asked. Dark circles were beginning to line his eyes, and he seemed to be in a perpetual state of exhaustion. Nonetheless, he glared at me with a sharp awareness that was fascinating and disconcerting.

"My friends have kept me busy," I admitted at last. *Friends* was a word Rose had used when we were at one of the clubs. I didn't know what it meant, and the definition on the holos was confusing.

He stepped back, looking pleased.

"You consider them your friends?" he asked.

I made a noncommittal noise.

"That was faster than any Rookie has made friends before," he continued. "And I've been here for... for a while."

Before I could ask what he meant, he took my hand, sliding his thumb up my arm to remove the bandage.

90

His eyes widened and he traced the tattoo, something seeming to light up in his expression.

His head snapped up to meet my gaze, with what could only be described as a smile on what I could see of his face.

Still I scowled and wrapped the gauze back around my arm.

"How did you see me last night? I'm pretty sure I would notice someone with yellow eyes," I snapped, changing the subject. His earnest expression faded, and he regarded me with a cold stare. I wished he was smiling again.

He pulled his hand back, maybe a little too fast.

"My eyes aren't yellow." It was a tone I'd heard before, from my teachers back in the city, a tone that meant the conversation was over.

He came back the next night anyway.

And the next.

And the next.

And the next.

CHAPTER 10

"Ray-venn," came a sing-song voice. "Time to get up."

I forced my eyes open and blinked at Rose, groggy.

Her pink hair was pinned into loose curls— she put them up like that before bed every night— and her hands hung loosely at her sides. She yawned, shifting on her feet to look at me.

"Time for training," she murmured, a sleepy quality to her voice. I pushed myself out of bed and followed her without comment. I'd slept through the night for the first time in days, so I was well rested, but in a strange mood.

The word *training* didn't sink in until we had reached the gym.

It wasn't really a gym so much as a giant warehouse. Pieces of equipment dangled from chains on the rusted metal beams, a thin layer of sand coating the cement floor.

Light filtered through the dirty windows, coating half the room in a yellow glow and plunging the other half in darkness. A vinyl mat was laid out on one side in the room, a series of boxing gloves and mouthguards laid out in neat rows. Wooden crates were scattered in every corner, some of them pried open.

"Woah," I said, turning in a circle to take it all in. "It's very... big."

The only people here this early were Obsidian, a girl with dark skin and neon green hair, and... Shadow. I supposed this would explain his absence last night.

Obsidian and Rose had gotten into an intense argument a couple days ago, and they were both still mad about it. Rose did a better job of hiding it, though, offering a polite smile that was only a little smug.

Obsidian was scowling but didn't otherwise betray his anger. He moved to partner with her in silence.

"You okay, Obsidian?" Rose tilted her head. "Picking up a bit of hostility here."

I thought he would snap at her; really I did. Instead, he closed his eyes for a long moment, opened them, and nodded as Shadow offered to partner with me.

I picked up the helmet and put it on the way I thought it should go, but it dug into my skin in all the wrong ways.

"That's on backward," Shadow chuckled, reaching out and fixing it. I held still, memorizing the way he put it on. He snapped the chin strap on and seized my wrist before I could pull away.

"This won't be what you think it'll be," he warned. "I know how impulsive you are; I know that, if this were a real fight, you'd probably lose. Hell, you'd probably die. Use that brain of yours, Rookie. Prove me wrong."

Challenge accepted, you presumptuous creep.

I fit the mouthguard to my teeth and put the boxing gloves on, sliding my thumbs through the smaller parts and feeling my hands curl inside the heavy fabric.

Shadow's gaze scanned my body, noting various weaknesses and liabilities he could use against me.

"Go," he breathed, and the moment the word left his mouth everyone moved, kicking up the sand on the floor.

I swung my arm as hard as I could and felt my glove connect with Shadow's hand. He pushed my hand back and I fumbled for balance.

"Sloppy," he observed, before sweeping my feet out from under me.

My back hit the ground hard. I scrambled back up and punched his jaw.

Shadow stood, solid as a brick, as though my hit had done nothing, before twisting my arm behind me and pinning it to my back. I grit my teeth to muffle the hiss I let out. He chuckled. "What did I say about thinking ahead?"

This made me angry. I hit him again, on his left temple. This time there was a reaction.

He took a step back, a smile spreading across his face.

Out of the corner of my eye, I saw Rose punch Obsidian's nose, heard the low, vicious words he spat at her.

I felt Shadow hit my stomach, taking advantage of my momentary distraction.

"Don't let your attention be diverted," he advised. "Not for a moment."

I lunged, aiming a kick at his crotch, but he danced out of my way.

"Honestly, Rookie," he let out a breathy chuckle. "You'd be dead by now."

Almost before he finished, I charged forward, making like I was going to hit his temple again, then changed direction mid-swing and hooked upward, hitting him right in the throat. He staggered back and

I aimed hits at his eye and then his nose. Neither of them landed, but I kept moving anyway, springing back up every time he managed to knock me down; which happened more times than I cared to admit.

Shadow was on the floor for the first time in what was either me finally getting the hang of it or a wild bout of luck, and I planted my foot on his chest, pushing down to try and keep him on the ground.

His eyes sparkled and he started laughing.

"How *dare* you–" I started, pressing harder.

And the earth began to shake.

A mask of calm slipped over Shadow's face, and for a moment he looked like someone else.

"Bombs," he said, springing up from where I'd been holding him as if I wasn't even there. "Run!" His voice pushed the others into a sprint. "Into the lower levels!"

His hand was firm around my wrist, dragging me along until I tripped.

"Raven! Come *on!*"

I obeyed, trying to focus enough to keep up with him. But my mind was racing.

The look on his face... I'd seen it before. On someone else, but who had it been? Someone at that party?

Why did I care? He was a random boy who looked nice and sometimes danced with me.

He was just one of the Crows that Rose listed, one of the ones who I had just completely forgotten. Who I shouldn't have completely forgotten.

But something still didn't seem right, and my head was spinning as I sprinted to the elevator.

CHAPTER 11

I was scared.

Bombs were something used in the Dark Ages. There had to be at least forty laws warning against and forbidding the use of them.

The Conurbation wasn't supposed to have them, but I guessed they also weren't supposed to have cars. Or guns.

Seven people were in this glass tube aside from me, and the lights flashed once, twice, three times.

And then we went into freefall. Obsidian barked a laugh as the yelp escaped me and moved so I could hold the rail. His nose was crooked and must've hurt like hell, but the bleeding had stopped. He caught me looking and shifted his wiry frame, but just like that, it was over. I waited until everyone left to walk out, barely registering the four other elevators before I entered the room.

The space was a vast chamber, lined with alcoves. Far above, conveyor belts laden with food and emergency supplies sped along. I could see a small infirmary before Rose, Crystal, and Dove made their way to one of the cramped bedrooms, with Dove motioning for me to follow.

The ceiling was low and the space was small. Most of it was taken up by a large mattress, and another one above it. A string of lights was mounted above each bed, with five pillows on both cushions. White comforters were folded in half over the flat sheet. Sheer curtains were hung over the entrance, and it had a pleasant, cozy feel. This did not make me feel any better.

We wound up rooming with six other girls.

I didn't have time to take in any of them except for Jackie, who was gaunt and deathly pale, a bandage wrapped around her shoulder.

I was crying; I had never been so scared in my entire life. Other than that, I was silent.

Another awful tremor shuddered throughout the room, and I pressed myself harder against the wall, imagining the ceiling collapsing and crushing everyone to death.

What was going on up there? How much closer to the shelter were the bombs getting?

The little shelf behind me had strange, cube-like objects, some kind of bound paper. I pulled one off to examine the blue-and-gold cover. *Parallel Lives,* it read. *Plutarch.*

I tapped Jackie's arm and she turned to look at me.

"What's this?" I asked, breaking the silence.

"A book," she replied, fingering the binding. "I haven't seen one of these in a while."

I poked the cover.

"How do I activate it?"

Jackie laughed and tugged on the top, pulling it open and revealing the worn yellow pages.

"Woah," I breathed, picking it up and savoring the whisper of paper beneath my fingers. "Should I read it?"

Jackie smiled and punched my shoulder.

"You look like someone served you the sun and moon on a platter," she teased.

My lips tugged into an absentminded smile, but I was already reading.

It wasn't long before a loud rumble broke the silence. The lights flickered and went out.

CHAPTER 12

As I waited for my eyes to adjust, I kept still. I wasn't afraid of the dark, but something about the silence, the stillness of it, made me tremble.

Hours passed and I heard the other girls breathing evenly, asleep.

Then someone grabbed my hand.

Out of reflex, my leg kicked out and connected with someone's chest. Solid, muscular.

There was a quiet grunt, decidedly male.

"Sorry," Shadow wheezed. "Should've let you know it was me." I could see his glowing gold eyes slicing through the dark, strange and distant like the stars I watched each night.

"Shadow?"

"Come with me," he whispered.

I slid off the bed and followed him.

We went into a small room with weak light, perhaps a maintenance closet.

He was wearing the same black outfit as he was when we were training. I sighed, crossing my arms.

"This had better be good."

Shadow studied me, an awkward expression on his face. I guessed that he hadn't expected me to follow him.

"Well," he stammered. I had never heard him sound nervous. "I figured you might–" he cleared his throat. "Might want to talk." I looked at him, furrowing his brow. "Or, you know, train. Because you're a Rookie, and all."

"Practice what?"

"Not kicking people every time they come up to you, for instance."

"Sorry."

"No," he said, smiling. "You're not."

"Okay," I challenged. "Tell me how to punch someone."

"Wow. I knew you were a lot of things, but violent wasn't really on the top of my list."

"That's what you people want down here, isn't it." It wasn't a question. I stared into his eyes until he looked away. When he didn't answer, I scoffed. "If I had known you weren't going to tell me anything, I would have just stayed in bed."

"Didn't look like you were doing much sleeping," Shadow commented.

"So, should I go back, or should I hit you and see if I do it right?"

He laughed, taking a few steps forward.

"You're sloppy," he said. "Easy to beat."

"If you don't answer directly," I warned, "I'll just assume you want me to hit you."

"If you somehow manage to hit me hard enough, there is a high probability that you'll get in trouble."

"Why? Know someone powerful?"

He seemed to find this incredibly amusing; an insufferable grin tugging at his lips.

"God, if only you knew," he laughed, and I could sense him fighting back a weird hiss in his voice.

I *knew* that voice. *Where did I hear that voice before?*

"Okay," he relented. "Training. Try and hurt me."

"Really?" I asked, doubtful at his sudden change in heart. "Cause that's a *little bit* different from what comes to mind when I hear the word *training*. Also, you *just said* I shouldn't *do that.*"

"Wow," Shadow said without a hint of amusement. "You *do* listen! Sometimes."

"Oh, and he's a wise guy." He grinned at this and reached out as if he might tousle my hair, pulling back at the last second.

"Come on," he pressed. "Show me what you can do. I won't block."

I closed my eyes, taking a deep breath, and aimed to catch him just below the rib cage with a swift kick to his stomach. He wouldn't think of me as weak, oh no— I'd show him.

A tiny spark jumped off my foot, then another.

I'd.

The sparks grew longer, brighter, hotter. Maybe it was my imagination, maybe I was losing my mind, probably I was just tired.

Show.

Now I had miniature lightning bolts dancing up along my leg and my foot connected with his chest.

Him.

CHAPTER 13

Shadow crumpled, gasping for air. His hands curled on his throat, dry, hacking coughs clawing out of his mouth. The smell of burning flesh curdled in my nose.

"Shadow!" I cried, reaching out and seizing his shoulder.

Doubled over, he pointed a shaking finger to the counter, where an L-shaped device lay.

An inhaler.

Shadow had asthma like I used to have, and I'd probably set him off by kicking him in the chest. Twice. Something heavy and cold pressed against my chest as my fingers prickled with energy, energy to help, to heal. So different from what I'd felt moments earlier.

Why he didn't have surgery to get it removed at an early age was beyond my understanding, but maybe he didn't have the same luxury I had when it came to something like this. Perhaps he was born out of the country, away from the Medicals.

I snatched the inhaler off the counter, ignoring the tingling sensation in my fingers, and pushed it into his hand.

He pressed it to his mouth and drew in two shuddering puffs, his coughing under control at last.

Then he turned to offer me a halfhearted attempt at a smile, gold eyes flickering.

"Thanks," he said in a hoarse voice. "You must've kicked me harder than I thought..." He cleared his throat, smoke slipping between his lips. *Smoke.*

"Is that—"

"From the inhaler," he interrupted me. "What—" Shadow coughed. *"Shadow?"*

I shifted, tense. Should I press him more on the smoke? Or was I still seeing things?

"You said I could call you whatever," I shrugged. "Shadow seemed appropriate."

His eyes sparkled the way they did when he was smiling.

"Why did you bring me here?" I asked after a pause. "Be honest."

106

Shadow sank down against the wall, rubbing his face. His eyes were sort of blank, like he was in shock, but something about him seemed energized now, more energized than I'd seen him in a long time.

"I..." He was quiet, thinking. Or maybe processing, I didn't know. "I like talking to you." Another pause. "But also," he admitted, "because this scares me a little."

I sat down next to him and put my head on his shoulder. "Only a little, though, right?"

"Only a little," he agreed, resting his cheek on top of my head.

I could have stayed like that forever.

"You should go," Shadow said after a long silence. "Before–"

The soft pad of bare feet approaching sounded nearby, followed by a whisper: "Raven?" This voice belonged to Rose.

"Before that," he finished.

I hesitated, pushing myself to my feet, then bent down to help him up.

His grasp was gentle and light, the way it had been when we had danced. And then I remembered the punch to my stomach, like a brick had been hurled into my gut. This boy– I had to admit, if only to myself –was intriguing. His hands– how could they caress my arm like a breath of wind one moment and leave me doubled over in pain the next? Whatever it was about him, he had my attention, for now at least, I told myself as I walked back to the alcove.

I lay down and sleep came for me.

I dreamed tonight, but it was a memory. Something resembling a memory, at least.

"The First Death of Earth began with World War Five," the hologram droned. At the front of the room sat my teacher, her lips a tight line.

Serpents writhed up the walls, bugs crawling up the legs of my desk. Occasionally, a snake would slide up my desk and bite me. Calf, ankle, neck, wrist. Bugs scuttled along my spine.

My hands twitched. "Every country had something different to say about the state of Planet Earth. Every country was being torn apart. Out of the chaos and darkness, a shining city was born, a ray of light thrust from the heavens. The New Order, soon to be known as the Conurbation, created a set of rules known as the Code. The citizens of this fledgling world, this newfound paradise, were able to find a world of peace and prosperity, and mankind would never be threatened by its own existence again—"

The high-pitched whine of metal on stone pierced the air.

The class jumped and looked around as I pushed away from my desk, backing away, but I didn't know from what: the creatures or the people.

CHAPTER 14

My eyes were open before I was awake.

Those moments and countless more, weaknesses in my composure, had cost me. Those little rebellions; the comments on my report cards about my disobedience; my outbursts; my anger; that's what landed me here. And there was nothing I could do about it now.

If I had just kept my mouth shut; if I had managed to control my temper, maybe I could still be living my old life right now. Perhaps I wouldn't be so afraid.

Then again, maybe not.

"If I stay down here for another minute," someone above hissed, teeth clenched, "I swear I will lose my freaking mind."

I was pretty sure she wasn't the one with a fear of physical contact and an inability to sleep near other people. All I could feel the night before was heat radiating off the other girls despite the air conditioning that vibrated from above and the sweat and I couldn't tell whose it was and bodies pressing against each other even when I pushed myself against the stone wall. It was a nightmare, not to mention the fact that every five minutes another bomb struck, and I couldn't sleep because every time, there was a chance we all died. The nightmares didn't help.

"You're not the only one," Jackie grumbled, dark circles under her eyes. She looked thinner than usual. Enough that I wondered when she'd last eaten as she rummaged in her bag for the brick of green dye and a bottle of water.

"Okay," Rose chimed in out of nowhere, smiling. "I would like some yogurt."

I stared at her for a minute before she giggled.

Jackie shook her head, pulling a lock of hair to the side and applying the green. She threw a towel on her shoulders

"I'm bored," Rose said. "And I still want yogurt."

"Good for you," Dove muttered.

Jackie pulled out a deck of cards and a handful of capitals.

"Rose," she said with a dramatic flourish of her hand, "Naomi, Jade, Raven, wanna play BS?"

111

"I'll watch, thanks though," I murmured, still rubbing the sleep from my eyes.

They sat in a small circle around the capitals, dealing cards.

"I have an ace," Jackie announced, putting her card down.

"I have a two," Naomi claimed.

"BS!" the girl called Jade yelled. Naomi sighed and picked up the two cards in the pile.

"I have a three," Rose cheered. "And I really want yogurt."

"I have a four," Jade said, ignoring her.

"Five," Jackie replied.

"Six."

"Seven! But my favorite number is five and—"

"Eight."

"Peanut butter!" Rose cried. I jumped at the volume of her voice.

"Nine"

"Ten."

"BS!" Jade called.

Naomi swore at her and picked up the pile.

"Jack."

"BS," Rose sang.

"Take it," Jade replied, smirking. Rose sighed tragically and took the single card. I watched, trying to figure out how the game worked.

"Attention," the cool voice of Fas echoed through the room, quiet yet carrying to the farthest corner. All noise stopped, as if there was some kind of vacuum. "Everyone please report to the alcove in the back of the room." He sounded uncharacteristically calm, serene, even; despite the slight sag to his shoulders and the deep bags under his eyes; as he watched everyone as they began to make their way to the far alcove on the left wall.

It opened up into a large, stone room.

The table had a glass top with a glowing hologram, a model of the Conurbation city. Buildings flickered in neat rows, the smallest ones on the outside, then it grew gradually into a pyramid shape. The center had the tallest buildings, where the government functions were. The wall surrounding it dwarfed even the tallest in the city. The greenhouses dotted the outer ring of the state, the Forbidden Sector a thin strip just outside the greenhouses. Information inscribed above the country floated in green letters, some in languages I didn't recognize.

Beside the city was a detailed map of the sewer systems, with scrawled notes on which boats would best navigate it and where the guards were located.

I stared at it, wanting to touch it and not wanting to at the same time.

Rose tugged me down into the seat next to her, and I braced myself for a plan.

CHAPTER 15

"The Forbidden Sector was our home," Fas said. "In case you hadn't guessed yet, it is gone now."

A beat of silence.

"What do we do?" I don't know who asked the question, but it hung in the air, waiting for a response.

Fas looked down, then up again. "We leave." His voice came out quieter than usual, more tired. "There's nothing we can do aside from that. We lost."

"What do you mean 'we lost?'" I was standing now, defiance roaring in my veins. It felt good. But, slowly, every pair of eyes in the room turned to me, and I wished I hadn't said anything at all. I sat back down. "How could we have *lost?*" I added in a softer voice.

The gazes cast my way turned pitiful. Again, I wished I hadn't spoken.

"We have nowhere to go," Fas said. "We've lost most of our weapons, all of our food, and our medical supplies. I'm sorry, Raven, but there's nothing we can do." He didn't *look* sorry. He looked empty, but otherwise cool and collected. Maybe the two were the same with him.

"What are the next generation of Defects going to do, then?" Apollo's question surprised me. I glanced his way, but he was staring straight at Fas, carefully keeping his eyes away from anyone else in the room.

Fas spread his hands. "Fend for themselves. Figure it out on their own." Apollo's eyes flickered, but he let Fas finish. "We won't be here. There is nothing we can do."

Apollo nodded once and did not protest. However, when the questions changed and conversation broke out throughout the room, he left.

"I need you to be on my side right now."

"How am I supposed to side with you when you're leading these people to their deaths?"

The girl Fas was arguing with tossed her long golden hair over one shoulder and crossed her arms, glowering.

"Could you keep your voice down?" he hissed.

"No. You have no idea what you're doing—"

"I have more of an idea than the rest of them."

"You're going to get us all *killed,* Fas—"

"That's *enough.* There's nothing else we can do." She tried to speak again, but he talked over her. "Conversation over. Understood?"

She pursed her lips and walked away, dragging a hand through her hair.

"This makes no sense," I said, picking at my lip. "Where are we even going?"

"Outside." Jackie glanced up at the ceiling. "He's talked about it before, but it's supposed to be a last resort."

"I'd say the entirety of the Forbidden Sector getting bombed into oblivion calls for a last resort, wouldn't you?" Apollo leaned against the wall, arms crossed, staring at the ceiling.

"No one *asked* you," Rose snapped.

"Please," he scoffed, "as if *you* wait for people to ask your opinion before sharing."

"Actually, you know what," Rose raised her voice so everyone could hear, turning a smug stare to meet Apollo's eyes. "I think there's something everyone deserves to know about *two of our own members,* something they *themselves* have not yet... *shared.*" Apollo pushed off the wall, face going white, and Rose smirked at him. She mouthed a word I didn't catch. His cheeks went a few shades paler. "Dunno why you freaked out so much earlier," she added. "It isn't like you care."

He paused, as if considering a defense, but he just closed his eyes. "You're right, I don't. What I do care about is you holding— holding *that* over my head. Stop."

"I'll stop holding it over your head when you tell everyone." She smiled. "Because then I won't be able to anymore."

"It's— Fine." Apollo scowled. "Not as though it's going to matter anyway."

"What do you mean?" He flicked his eyes in my direction, not expecting me to cut in.

"I mean we're going to *die,* Raven."

"You know what?" Rose pushed him. "Shut up. She doesn't *need* that."

He raised his eyebrows. "She *asked* a *question.*"

"She just got here! If someone said something like that to you—"

"I wouldn't care." The corners of his lips pulled up slightly in a bitter smile. "Because I wasn't a little kid, and neither is she."

"Come on, Raven, we're leaving." Rose wrapped her hand around my upper arm and started to drag me off, towards Jackie.

"Good riddance," Apollo muttered. Rose kicked him in the shin, called him something I didn't understand, and took me away, shaking her head.

CHAPTER 16

The sun was setting as we ran up the metal stairs, all the footsteps too loud. We left with whatever we could carry, whatever was left, stone walls flying by.

The Forbidden Sector was in smoldering ruin, buildings lying in chunks in the road. The air was too thick and too dusty, small fires flickering in piles of treasured possessions. Smoke still clogged my nose, and the little shops had long since collapsed.

Reddish sunlight filtered through the dust clouds in jagged slants, glancing off the shards of glass scattered throughout the streets.

In the center of it all was a manhole, the cover lying forgotten on one side. One by one, we slipped through. Jackie helped me get in, but it was up to me to let go and fall through.

Our route was through the main river of the sewers. I stepped out onto the stone floors, my boots splashing in the water. Damp bricks arched over my head; guttering lights mounted every hundred feet.

The boat was small, black, with a deck and cabin on it but nothing else. I was the thirteenth person to get on, gripping the railing so hard my knuckles turned white.

I sat down on the wooden floor, leaning against the side of the boat, between Rose and Jackie. The blonde girl stepped up, glancing over her shoulder, before sinking down and resting her head in Jackie's lap. A red pen rested in my lap, one of the first and last things I would ever own.

A black backpack rested between my feet, and I pulled the blanket tighter around my shoulders. In each bag was a flashlight, batteries, an emergency blanket, and a first aid kit, along with personal belongings. Mine had the nothing but the dress Shadow had given me what felt like forever ago. Everyone leaned against one side of the boat, with two or three people on each end and four people lying in the middle. Only the injured rested in the small room below deck. It would be a long night, and we would need sleep.

I was leaving. I swallowed twice, then clicked the pen on and started drawing on my arm, first coloring in the blank spaces on my tattoo that I could reach, then adding smaller designs up and down my forearm.

I'd waited my whole life to leave this place, and that now it was finally happening, I didn't know what to think. Rose took a lock of my hair and started to braid it. I let her do it for a while before pulling away. She let out a dismayed sound, poking my shoulder, but I ignored her.

Someone was singing softly to herself, a song that didn't belong to this language. It was a river of honey and a sea of stars and everything and nothing all at once. It was hateful and agonized, deeply sorrowful in a way that was somehow dark and furious. Her voice was a sultry, rich sound with a husky edge that resulted in a ravishing melody filled with passion and yearning. There was a mournful air to her tune, a painful desire for a life that had been stolen. I closed my eyes and listened.

With the rocking, the quiet roar of the river, the pleasant feeling of gliding along, the heaviness in my eyes, I fell asleep quickly.

For once in my life, I didn't remember my dreams.

CHAPTER 17

There was an icy hand around my arm, shaking me awake.

"It was very stupid of you," came the voice in my ear, "to leave as soon as you did. Get up, all of you."

"Do as he says," Fas said. His voice was even, but there was a bit of a strain there, enough of one that I glanced in his direction. His sister— the blonde— was on her knees on the ground, a gun trained on her head.

Somehow, I couldn't move. So I lay frozen on the floor of the boat until the man kneeling next me dragged me to my feet.

"Get up." His eyes narrowed and he punched me in the stomach, seized me by the hair to keep me standing, demanded to know what was wrong with me. When I didn't respond he called me an animal and threatened to cut my ears so they'd be normal.

And so I obeyed, my shaking knees barely supporting my weight.

We were lined up, shoulder to shoulder, our hands tied behind our backs, fabric stuffed into our mouths.

For a second, I thought I was going to die. Instead, I was blindfolded and led down a set of ancient wooden steps, and onto a platform, trying not to fall as it swayed back and forth. Someone lifted me into the back of a van.

I settled somewhere in the middle, murmuring a muffled apology when I tripped over someone's leg. The vehicle lurched forward without warning— I hit my head on the wall and lost consciousness.

The next thing I was aware of was the swaying movement of a car, but I was only aware for a few moments before closing my eyes again.

What followed was the falling sensation I sometimes got when I was falling asleep. Then my body slammed into something solid.

I was so shocked at the impact that my right arm didn't hurt at first. I was fine until I tried sitting up, when I fell back down, grinding my teeth to keep from crying out.

"You're 9729."

I pushed my heels into the floor and slid myself into a sitting position, cradling my arm to my chest.

There was a shadowy figure in the hallway about two cells over, fingers laced around the bars. Hers wasn't the threatening stance I was used to— no, she was just curious. "Well," she prodded, "aren't you?"

"Unfortunately." This voice belonged to Apollo. A pause. "Why don't you run along now, before you get yourself in trouble?"

"I won't." She bounced on the balls of her feet a little and I narrowed my eyes through the thick haze of pain. That was *not* normal. "This is an interrogation."

Apollo did not respond.

A second shadow joined the first— male, judging from the height and build— and wrapped his hand tightly around her arm. "9733, let's go. If you get another infraction—"

"I'm just—" She caught herself. "Fine. Call 9880. I'm not going to be held responsible for twenty-nine escaping."

There were a few minutes of silence after they left where I could try and process what I'd just heard. I could even make a bold attempt at seeing who was in the cells across the hall, which failed. It was too dark, save for the dim light coming from the next hallway.

Two shadows soon replaced the original, though, so I turned my attention back over there.

These new guards, unlike the younger girl who'd just come through, were silent in their vigil.

This did not escape Apollo, who first coughed awkwardly and then decided his time would be best spent annoying them.

"Not very talkative, are you?" he said.

Neither guard moved.

"I heard something recently." His tone was very conversational, more so than I'd ever heard him. "I heard that, after your Finding, they take your brain out and replace it with a computer. That true?"

It occurred to me that he might have a death wish.

Still, neither one of them moved.

"Can I take your silence as a yes?" He stood. "What would happen if I—" There was a clattering sound as he kicked the bars. "What would you do then? How about if I tried to escape?" He kicked the bars again, and one of the guards stepped forward. "If I stole your gun while your back was turned?" The man grabbed his wrist.

"Now you listen here, little boy." He reached to his side and pulled something out, the cool *shick* of metal on plastic echoing in the otherwise silent hallway. A gun, maybe? "If you keep acting up, we're going to have to deal with you, and at some point, if you refuse to cooperate, you're going to die."

Apollo let out a short breath that might have been laughter. "Oh, I dare you. Shoot me. Solve your six-year-old problem right here, right now."

It occurred to me that he *definitely* had a death wish.

"I don't want to shoot you," the man continued in a reasonable tone of voice. "Chances are, you don't want to be shot."

"Now, let's not make bold assumptions."

The man let out a long breath. "I know you're trying to get under my skin, Nathan. It won't work."

"Funny," Apollo said, "that's exactly what the other guards said."

"I'm not *other guards*."

"The other guards also said that." His tone of voice implied he'd done this plenty of times before. I had to admit, I wished I'd known how to aggravate my teachers like he probably could, wish I'd had the right words at the right time. "Let me guess, this prison is also higher security? It's got better staff? More weapons? I'm intimidated." This was the most I'd ever heard him talk at one time. "I do appreciate the iron bars, though. Maybe you should add a whole wing just made of the stuff." He did an exaggerated wave of his hands that I managed to catch despite the darkness. "That way, when I escape, you could at least say you tried?"

Someone in a nearby cell laughed under their breath.

"Keep it up. I wasn't going to shoot you, Nathan, but I will take you to solitary."

"I'm terrified," Apollo said flatly. "I might just faint."

"The Overseer is here as well. He's excited to meet you."

Apollo paused at this; caught unprepared for the first time since I'd met him, perhaps the first time in his life. He recovered a moment later. "Impressive. Think he'll kiss me hello?"

The guard's face didn't change as he rammed something large and blunt into Apollo's chest.

"Behave," he ordered. Apollo staggered back; he hadn't been expecting that. "Unless you want to get tazed. I've heard how fond you are of electrocution."

Apollo didn't say anything. Getting confident, the guard stepped forward, dragging his gun or his baton or whichever new weapon he had now along the bars. This was his mistake.

I didn't see what happened, but it wasn't hard to guess. One second the guard was upright, leaning towards the man in the cell before him, the next he was doubled over, holding his face with one hand while the other hung by his side, fingers bent at awkward angles.

His companion stopped a uniformed official and gestured, the first movement she'd made this whole time. "Get him to a Medical."

The official nodded. "Graduating class?"

"Mmh."

"This the one they tested the new conditioning program on?"

The woman nodded, and the official huffed a laugh.

"Gotcha. Come on, kid, let's go. I'll send someone to take care of 9729."

"Thank you," the woman said. Then she turned to Apollo. "I'd behave if I were you—"

"Of course *you* would. I, however, happen to be Defective. Defective people tend to— oh, I don't know— *not* behave?"

"As I was saying." Her cold gaze flicked up to examine him, unamused. "I would behave if I were you, so I could stand a fighting chance of not going to the Correction Center."

This seemed to get through to him, at least for a moment. "Doesn't matter. I'm going either way."

"Maybe," she ground out, getting irritated now, "if you don't hurt people, they'll be *nicer* to you."

"You're the first person I've ever met who used the phrase 'nice' when talking about the Correction Center." His demeanor was pretty relaxed for someone who was awaiting punishment. "And, again, doesn't matter."

129

The woman shifted her weight, glanced at the ceiling, and didn't say anything else.

It dawned on me that Apollo and the guard he'd just injured probably weren't that far apart in age. It dawned on me that, had things gone differently, their places might have been reversed.

CHAPTER 18

The person in the cell next to me had been scratching at something on the ground for about an hour now and I was ready to *rip the bars out of the wall and use them as a weapon on whoever it was* if they didn't stop. My arm was throbbing, my head hurt. I just wanted some sleep, maybe. Silence, at the very least.

They paused in their scraping and leaned the side of their head against the wall.

From what I could see, the person was male, with hair that was either blue or green or gray; unhelpful. But he *had* stopped. He had finally, finally—

The sound of nails on stone screeched through the air again and I had to bite my tongue to keep from growling.

"Do you *mind?*"

He turned in my direction, stopping what he was doing in his surprise.

Fas. His aquamarine gaze was unmistakable, due in part to the fact that his eyes were *literally glowing.* He must've gotten a surgery or special contacts; maybe he'd done the same thing Shadow did to make his irises look like molten gold.

"Your arm is broken," Fas observed.

I gasped in mock bewilderment. "You don't say!"

"Sorry." His voice held a note of amusement.

"Whatever. Listen." I edged closer to his cell. "Wanna tell me what you were doing?"

He blinked. "Doing... When?"

"For the past hour?" This didn't seem to help. "Were you trying to get out? If you were, I hate to break it to you, but usually you can't dig holes in stone the way you can with sand. I know; I've tried—"

"You've tried digging a hole in stone before?" Now he was grinning. "With your bare hands?"

"That's what I just said. Pay attention." I leaned my head against the wall. "Also, this discussion is not about me. What were *you* doing?"

"Just trying to figure some stuff out."

"Figure some stuff out," I repeated in as flat a voice as I could muster. "Out of curiosity, have your nails broken yet? I want to go to sleep at some point maybe."

Instead of replying, he sighed and glanced out into the hallway. "It looks like we're going to be here awhile."

"Do you state the obvious often?"

"Only sometimes." He edged a tad closer to me; the movement was almost imperceptible, but I caught it nonetheless.

"If we're going to be here awhile, does that mean you're going to stop scratching the floor?"

Fas allowed himself a small smile, the rough equivalent of laughter, and I got a tiny spark of happiness. I'd make him laugh for real one day, I promised myself. Maybe it'd be super embarrassing and I could make fun of him.

He cleared his throat. "Can I, uh, see your arm?"

"Why?" I narrowed my eyes and moved my hand back, grinding my teeth against the pain. I was pretty sure I'd broken more than just my forearm— it felt like little knives were jabbing into my elbow, my

133

wrist, and each of my knuckles, and I couldn't turn my palm upwards. I was also starting to feel dizzy.

"Just want to make sure it isn't broken too badly."

I regarded him one more time, making sure he knew I was suspicious, before picking up my right arm with my left and showing it to him.

Fas touched my fingers gingerly— they were already swollen— and then my palm, touching his thumb and middle finger together around my wrist. Then he squeezed.

"Hey–" I protested, trying to pull away.

He only held me more firmly, making me gasp.

His palm began to glow blue, spreading out through his hand in jagged patterns— veins, I realized. His pupils flared, becoming pointed and catlike, growing brighter and brighter until it hurt to look at him.

I had to bite my lip to keep from screaming. My arm hurt so badly at that moment that I didn't register the sharp sensation of my lip splitting open, didn't even know I had broken skin until I felt a bead of blood trickle down my chin.

The flesh of my arm went transparent, my bones glowing a pale bluish green; it was like some kind of demented X-ray. There was only one break, starkly visible as it bent and fused together. And then the pain was gone, and the glow faded.

I stared for a moment before opening my mouth— to scream, to call the guards, to ask him what happened— I didn't know. All I did know was that what I had just seen was not natural, it was not human.

Fas clenched my arm, eyes wide. "Don't. I was *not* supposed to do that. And you're welcome," he added, "by the way."

He removed his hand and I considered trying to scream again.

"What— what *was* that?" I whispered instead, barely able to speak because every instinct screamed at me to *run*, to get as far away from whatever just happened as possible.

"It doesn't matter." Any emotion had left Fas's face, and his voice had taken on a cold quality. "Don't tell a soul. I can wipe your memory."

I wanted to say something to ease the tension in the air, so I said, "You see, ordering me not to tell anyone might just guarantee—" At the look he gave me, though, I trailed off. It wouldn't have worked anyway; my voice was shaking as badly as my hands.

"I'm being serious."

I sighed. "Aren't you always?"

Fas made an exasperated noise in the back of his throat. "Raven." It was just my name, but he managed to make it sound like a whole entire lecture. When I didn't reply, he shook his head. "Listen, I know you're probably freaked out right now; most people are. But I *need* you to keep it a secret. Please."

"I—" I pressed my lips together when it became apparent there was no arguing with him. "Fine."

"I'm holding you to that." He leaned his head against the wall. "And don't say anything when they come to get me. They aren't going to be happy I did that for you."

"They?" I wasn't sure why we were whispering now, but it made me uneasy.

"Just..." He forced a smile. "Know what? Don't worry about it. It's going to be alright."

If I was uneasy before, I was on the edge of freaking out again now. "What?"

The door to his cell rattled and swung open, two guards looming in the threshold.

They turned their flashlights in our direction, and I hissed despite myself; temporarily blinded. When my eyes adjusted, I fell silent.

One of them was horrifically generic, a bland face, dull brown eyes, common brown hair. This man had been torn down and built back up with a new face. If I ever would have recognized him before, I wouldn't now. The other was older. His eyes were a cold, bleak gray color, and he had silver streaks in his hair, age starting to reverse his gene therapy.

"I think you know what you've done," the older one said.

Fas's breathing slowed, almost deliberately, like he was trying to trick them into thinking he was calm. Then he stood, offering his hands to them. They weren't gentle when they seized him and dragged him off towards the light at the end of the hallway; the younger one kicked him. And all I could do was watch.

I didn't like this feeling; the heaviness in my chest, the sensation of the floor giving way beneath me. But I was dealing with it more and more often, and there was nothing I could do but take a deep breath, let it out, and wait.

Time seemed to slow as I watched the leader; *my* leader; the key to our escape, dragged to his torture and possible death.

I curled into a tight ball, drawing my knees into my chest and allowing my eyes to wander. A light flickered on, casting a weak light, and a flash of movement caught my eye.

The person in the cell next to Fas's was Obsidian, who currently had his face in his hands. Next to him was Apollo, recently returned from whatever punishment they'd given him.

"You okay?" This was Obsidian. I had to strain to listen.

"Fine." Apollo.

Obsidian let out a long breath. "You have to be more careful."

"Obsidian." This sounded like a synonym for *stop.*

"I'm serious. You're going to get yourself killed, and—" His voice gave out and he removed his hands from his face. "You can't keep *doing* this. We aren't— we aren't *in* Secondary anymore. This is the real world, we're not teenagers anymore." He hesitated, as if considering something else to say, but fell silent.

"I'm sorry." These were not the words I was expecting. The words I was expecting were *are you done* or *don't lecture me* or *I'm not a child.* Then again, as brothers, he and Obsidian were close.

"It's fine." It was, very clearly, *not* fine. Obsidian lowered his voice further, and I could no longer hear what he was saying. Obsidian was leaning against the bars now, holding Apollo's hands. "We'll get out of here soon. It'll be fine, we'll be fine. Just... just behave? And we can be together for the *rest of our lives.* We can't do that if you get yourself killed."

...

Be... together? That wasn't something brothers said. Was it? *That isn't something brothers say.*

And that's when I realized they weren't brothers at all.

CHAPTER 19

I had fallen asleep by the time the guards returned, carrying Fas between them.

They flung him unceremoniously into his cell and slammed the door. He hit the wall at an awkward angle before slumping to the ground and not moving. Was he unconscious?

"Fas," I whispered, leaning forward and shaking his shoulder, before pulling back with a hiss. The bars must have been charged or something, because they burned my skin where my wrist touched them. But it didn't seem to bother Obsidian... Maybe he was just used to it? "Fas, wake up, please."

At first nothing happened. Then he made a tiny sound and opened his eyes. His throat bobbed. "Hi," he whispered.

"Are you okay? What did they...?" I trailed off, watching something flash green. "Did they put a tracker on you?"

He sighed. "No. They—" He lifted his hand.

A weak emerald glow illuminated his arm, revealing every detail.

His hand was prosthetic.

It was completely artificial, made of plastic and some kind of metal, a series of green lights flashing in order every couple of seconds. The prosthetic extended to his elbow, where metal met flesh in an awkward combination of nature and technology. My hand pressed against my mouth to keep me from making a sound.

It was metal. His hand was metal. They'd *cut off* his hand in compensation for what he'd done, what he'd done for *me*...

"Are you..." I wanted to say *are you okay,* but my voice gave out before the sentence finished. I'd wanted to come across as cool and collected as he normally did, but I just kept imagining the way they must've dragged him into that room, kept wondering whether he resisted.

"Raven," he said. "It's fine. I'm fine." He sounded tired. "Don't freak out."

"I'm not," I said stubbornly, resting my head on my knees so he couldn't see my face.

"I'm fine," Fas repeated. His gaze was absent. *Did they give him anesthesia?* Was that why he seemed so out of it, or was it because they didn't give him anything at all and he was hurt?

"I know," I said at last, deciding not to push it.

I leaned back against the stone wall, watching Fas withdraw to do the same. His gaze was downcast, and even in the darkness, I could see that his blank stare was directed at his hand. I bit my lip and let my hand come to rest on his shoulder.

Fas gave no indication that he noticed, but he relaxed a little, moving his hand from where it'd been in his lap.

I couldn't sleep— shocker there— so I stared at the wall, which was about as fun as it sounded.

And when, awhile later, the scent of salty air filled my nose, I stood, walking to the bars, following that strange, entrancing aroma.

I could *feel* it— an essence. Feel eddies and currents that pooled around my ankles, feel the salt-scented breeze.

My finger brushed the lock and it clicked open, tendrils of a soft, teal-blue color swirling around it. I cut a glance at Fas, but he was breathing evenly, asleep. This color was different than his— his whatever he could do— anyway. It was more like... more like the hologram of the ocean back at the Sector.

So I nudged the door open a crack, flinching at how it creaked. My lips parted and I pushed it a little more, marveling at my luck.

Then I slipped out, my hand curling on the door, and glanced around.

The rusted bars of my prison cell door were cool beneath my touch; I flinched when I realized what I was touching before relaxing when I eventually realized it wouldn't burn the way it usually did.

I expected the metal to creak; after all it was old, flecked with red-orange rust. But it was silent.

Fas was awake now, watching me, and his mouth formed one word: *go.*

I shook my head. No, not without everyone else. Fas's lips became a thin line and he mouthed it again.

Go.

"No," I breathed, aloud this time.

"Raven," he whispered, my name like a prayer. "Please—"

His eyes widened and he lunged for the bars, energy already crackling at his fingertips—

But it was too late to help me, too late as four guards seized me and started to drag me away. They didn't yield as I thrashed, twisting to glare into their eyes.

CHAPTER 20

In front of me, a severe-looking middle-aged man paced back and
forth. He was called the Overseer in pretense of guidance and wisdom;
he was much more like a dictator, for every decision he made during
his rule was final. The sentinels on either side of me kept a firm grip on
each of my arms.

This room was made of gray stone, the walls chipped and
weathered. In the middle of the room was a rickety table and a plastic
chair. It was this chair they shoved me into as the Overseer paused in
his pacing.

"Tell me why you're here," he growled.

"I've been wondering that myself, *sir*," I pushed as much sarcasm into the word *sir* as I could muster.

He stopped pacing to glare at me. I smirked.

"You picked the lock. Picking locks to prison doors is unauthorized."

"Funny, I thought picking locks to *any* doors here was unauthorized," I drawled, swinging my arm around the back of the chair.

"*That's entirely the point,*" he hissed, spit flying, before composing himself. "One hundred lashes," he spat. "Be grateful I'm not ordering to have your tongue cut out."

"You *destroyed* our *home.*"

"It should have been done a long time ago. That strip of buildings was a blight on our society and all that we stand for."

"I would argue that *you*, sir—"

"Now," the Overseer commanded, meeting my eyes with his own frozen gaze.

A female guard stepped forward, pulling a wicked-looking whip from her belt.

I paled.

The guards moved all at once. They stripped me of my prison clothes and strapped me, facedown, to the table before me, despite how I kicked and fought. There was a clean *snap* as the female guard cracked her whip just to scare me.

"Go," snapped the Overseer. He met my eyes. "Now."

For a moment, I felt nothing, just shock, then a line of fire snapped into being across my back. I whimpered.

"One."

She stared and raised the whip once more.

"Two."

I cringed.

"Three. Four. Five."

Tears streamed down my face; the pain was unbearable; but I refused to plead for help. I refused to grovel for mercy at the feet of these horrible monsters.

"Six. Seven. Eight."

I clenched my jaw and stared into the depths of the Overseer's cold, empty eyes, grimly determined not to let them see my pain.

"Nine."

I occupied myself with false promises of revenge. Although there was a low chance I would live to see them through, they brought me comfort.

"Ten."

I will make them pay.

"Eleven."

I will make them pay.

"Twelve."

It became like my heartbeat, over and over.

"Thirteen."

They will die *at my feet.*

Pain shot through my back and legs, burning. I stemmed my tears.

Sweat beaded on my neck and forehead.

"Fourteen."

My eyes rolled up into the back of my head and I passed out, pain throbbing even in my sleep; I faded in and out of consciousness for what seemed like an eternity.

"Thirty-four."

I suppressed a groan and closed my eyes again, burying my face in the crook of my arm. It was warm and dark, and even if I couldn't fall asleep, at least I could pretend.

"Forty-eight."

I tried not to make a sound at this. Only forty-eight lashes?

"Forty-nine."

"Fifty. Fifty-one-"

As a cry of anguish built up in my chest, an ember of *something* glowed in my heart, and I felt, I *sensed* a wave in the air around me, an ability I hadn't yet experienced but somehow understood. It was a ripple in the energy of the room, a charge somehow thrust from my own life force. The lights flickered.

Then they went out.

There was a split-second of confusion, and then the Overseer ordered,

"Continue."

There was a sharp *swish* as the rope was brought through the air. An involuntary yelp escaped my lips and I closed my eyes against the pain.

Again, I sensed the shockwave.

And I was aware that the whip did not hit me.

It had missed.

The Overseer growled.

"Try again," he commanded.

This time I heard the whistling of the whip in the air, directly on point. I could sense as it veered, seemingly on its own, off to the side at the last moment. I felt my muscles relaxing, although they trembled and despite the Overseer's glare.

It was over. No one had said it, but no one had to. It was over. At last, it was over. I could go back. I wasn't dead yet. They hadn't killed me. They could not kill me. I was stronger than them.

"Unstrap her," the Overseer ordered ungraciously, after a long, tense silence. "Take her to a Medical."

I staggered up, my skin screaming in agony. The guards stepped forward to grab my arms.

"No one touch me," I hissed, voice cracking. "I can walk."

They snarled but didn't argue, a sentry stalking on either side of me.

The walk back to my cell was excruciating.

Each step sent pain lashing down my back, my skin stinging from the dried-up tears on my cheeks.

My feet were sore from my week of nonstop movement. *Only a week?* I was still one of them; still one of the men and women who let their children be taken away, let their peers die for being different.

My fists clenched and I stared at my feet. A lock of my hair fell into my eyes and I scowled.

I might have looked like them, but that didn't mean I would ever, *ever* be anything like these sadists.

CHAPTER 21

I watched the guards stride off, drawing my knees into my chest and trying to ignore the pain. The medicine and ointment had helped, but it still hurt when I moved.

Fas was more still than I'd ever seen him, sitting on the cot with his elbows braced on his knees. His eyes were trained on the stone floor.

"They whipped you," he said in a voice so cold it sent chills down my spine.

I gave a curt nod.

He slipped off the cot in one fluid motion, crossing over to the bars as his expression softened.

"Raven, let me," he pleaded, lightly clasping my fingers. He moved his normal hand up my arm, a soft blue glow illuminating his fingertips.

I pulled away.

"Fas, I swear. If you're about to do the thing that got your arm chopped off, then don't touch me. Or I'll rip your good one off myself."

"Suit yourself." He shrugged. "It's gonna scar, though."

I crossed my arms, shooting him a nasty look. "Do you think I care?"

He shifted slightly, a ghost of a smile flickering across his face. "Just thought you might like to know."

As Fas eased himself back onto the bed, I glared at him.

He didn't even have to look at me, just bit his lip to keep from laughing. "What is it?"

"I don't need your help," I informed him.

"Thank you for letting me know."

I huffed a sigh and leaned forward to try and catch his eye. "When are we getting out of here?"

"I don't know." He lay down on the cot and draped his arm over his face. There was a beat of silence, two. Then he sat up. "Actually," Fas offered. "I can..." His eyes darted to the security camera and he looked down, the bright spark I'd seen only moments before dying down.

"You can what?"

"Nothing. Never mind."

There was a long silence during which I struggled to stand. First, I tried to use the bars, but it hurt to touch them; my palms came away bright red.

He watched as if debating whether to offer his assistance, but when I glared at him, he seemed to make up his mind.

I dropped onto the cot and crossed my legs, thinking about the people I'd met here.

I thought of Kitty, the girl who had taken me inside the abandoned buildings in the ghost towns in the Forbidden Sector. Where was she now? Had she made it outside the Barrier? Or was she here, in one of the cells? Was she dead?

I pushed the thought away.

Kitty was alive. Even if she wasn't, it didn't matter. People died all the time; statistically speaking, someone was probably dying right now.

But she remained in the back of my mind for the rest of the night.

CHAPTER 22

Apollo hadn't said anything all day; when prompted, he'd just nod or shake his head. His skin was pale, face slack, and he'd already been called away for 'questioning' three or four times now.

I occupied myself by talking to Fas; once he'd woken up. I didn't know what time it was, but I guessed it was afternoon; we'd been given food twice already.

"Do you know who's in the other cells?" I asked.

"Ah…" He turned to look. "Obsidian— I'm saying who's in the cells." This clarification came as Obsidian looked up from tracing patterns on the floor; Obsidian nodded and looked back down. "Apollo, Kampê, Rose, Opal… I can't see past him."

"Opal is a guy?"

Obsidian scoffed under his breath but didn't say anything.

"Why do you need to know?" Fas's gaze was inquisitive; I ignored this and ran my thumb along the corner of the cot.

"You don't know who else is here?"

"I don't," he said. "And I'd like to know why you're asking."

I waved my hand impatiently. "Just tell me."

"After Opal is Rose." He tilted his head, scrutinizing me. "After that, the entire facility is organized by age and sex."

"How do you know that?"

He gave me a Look; the kind my teachers used to give me when I asked a stupid question on purpose. But that wasn't a stupid question. At least, I didn't think it was.

Maybe it was; he had, after all, guessed what I was trying to figure out.

The arrival of my third meal was announced by the clattering of plastic on the stone floor. I stared at it for a moment, wondering if I could get it without trying to stand, before dragging myself to my feet and grabbing it.

It wasn't bad, as far as prison food went. It wasn't good. But it wasn't *bad,* it was just tasteless mush. I tried twice to start a conversation with someone before giving up and sitting back on the cot, running my fingers along the seam of the thin mattress.

In the middle of the night, I woke to Fas hissing my name at me.

"I have an idea," he whispered. "Do you remember how I healed your arm?"

"Vividly," I murmured, rubbing my eyes. Did he ever sleep? "And I thought we weren't talking about that?"

"I lied," he replied. "We're talking about it."

I rolled onto my back and looked at him upside-down, trying to ignore how the mattress crunched underneath me. "Okay. It was super freaking weird and I wish you didn't do it."

"Duly noted." He rubbed his metal hand with the real one. "But I am not asking for your opinion. I'm telling you about the idea I had. Remember?" His words could have been witty and sarcastic if there was any amusement in his voice, but he sounded dead. It made me shiver.

"Yes, Fas, my memory is fine."

"I can do the same thing to get us out of here."

I blinked. "Does it involve you getting killed?"

"Maybe," he said evenly.

I extended my hands toward him, palms-up. The blood was starting to rush to my head. "Then *why—*"

"Do you have any idea where we are?" He watched me, waiting for my response. There was none, so he proceeded. "There's a good chance I won't die. If I do, though, and seventy percent of the people who came here with us survive, then it's worth it."

"Not if the seventy percent of people who survive get themselves killed because you're not there to tell them which plants not to eat." He didn't respond. "I honestly don't even know why I'm arguing with you right now."

He laughed. "What else are you gonna do?"

I rolled my eyes.

"I know where everyone is."

I tilted my head at him. "Didn't you—"

"Listen, Raven." He rubbed his face. "Let's just assume— alright?— let's just assume that most of the things I say during the day are lies. Because we're being listened to. Does that make sense?"

"I guess so. How will I know when you aren't lying anymore?"

Fas gave me an amused look. "I'll let you know, I promise."

I wasn't sure I believed him.

CHAPTER 23

"Time to get up. Inmate count is in twenty minutes."

I dragged my fingers on the cot, momentarily forgetting where I was. My mouth was dry, my head was pounding, and my entire body ached. My back was even worse, though; the numbing ointment they'd put on me had worn off. *Numbing ointment...*

The realization hit me like a truck.

"9735, that means you, too."

I made a small sound and pushed myself into a sitting position. It was painfully slow, getting up, and I could feel the guard's eyes burning into my head.

"Glad you decided to join us." He snapped a pair of cuffs around my wrists; these hurt slightly less than it did to touch the bars. "You're the new Rogue, aren't you? Kinda scrawny for someone who's supposed to be dangerous."

I flushed, fists tightening. "Say that again and there'll be an 'accident' on the way to the breakfast hall."

He ignored me and shoved me forward, the heel of his palm landing right on one of the lashings. I yelped before turning to glare at him.

"Watch it."

"Or what," he mocked, "you'll rip my throat out with your pretty little hands?"

"Excellent idea, if it'll make you stop talking." I jumped at Apollo's voice and looked over. He was fidgeting with his handcuffs, as though he was halfheartedly trying to get out of them.

My guard leveled him a flat stare and steered me down the hallway. Just a little bit away from me, I saw Fas being taken in a separate direction.

"Now." His breath was in my ear, voice low and gravelly. I shuddered. "I've been assigned to keep you from causing any more trouble. I strongly advise you behave."

"Yes, sir. Whatever you say, sir."

My tone earned me a smack on the nape of my neck, right where the lash marks ended.

The breakfast hall was crowded, to say the least. The white-walled room was occupied by row upon row of gray-green tables, all full of people. But it was also silent.

A sea of faces greeted me— the Rogues who didn't make it to the Forbidden Sector. I don't know what I expected, then, but this wasn't it.

They looked normal. There was no dangerous gleam in their eyes, no missing pieces in their minds. It appeared as though I'd walked into a roomful of my classmates.

The Rogues in the Murder of Crows, however, I recognized immediately. Most of them had colored hair, some, like Jackie, were covered in tattoos, others had piercings. Everyone had *something*, though.

I noticed that, compared to everyone else I was standing by, I looked normal. Minus the purple color at the tips of my hair, which was starting to fade, my pale skin, and the dragon tattoo around my arm, I looked like everyone on the other side of the room.

And then I saw the little girl.

She was young, five or six.

Something about her, maybe the red, puffy eyes, maybe the fat tears rolling down her cheeks, maybe the guard who towered over her, *something* set my veins on fire.

So I stopped. In my tracks.

"What the hell do you think you're doing?" This question came from the guard escorting me.

"Where's the toilet," I said in a flat voice, not bothering to apologize.

I shouldered my way past Apollo and threw the door open, running into a stall and locking the door.

Deep breaths, deep breaths, deep—

I punched the wall.

The bathroom door swung open a moment later, and I pulled my legs up to my chest, pressing my mouth into my knee to keep the girl from hearing me. After she left, I washed the tears off my face.

When I returned, I was jostled into line with several other Rogues I didn't recognize. Some sort of oatmeal-looking food was plopped in my tray with an unappealing *splat* sound, and I moved over to where some of my friends were sitting.

I sat down next to Rose.

"Did you see the little girl?" I asked under my breath.

She nodded, turning to regard me with sorrowful blue eyes. "It happens more often than you'd think. I was a bit older, but... That little girl was me. And Jackie. Certainly Fas and Kampê. Well, Fas isn't a little girl, but..." She laughed, but it was strained.

I rubbed my neck, fingering the scabbed-over marks that stopped just above my shoulder blades.

After that, the conversation died, and I occupied myself with watching Opal. He had pale skin and white hair and brown eyes that were unnaturally dark compared to the rest of him, and he was playing with something. Little metallic flashes glinted from his hand from time to time before he put it on the table.

A key.

I drew in a sharp breath. "How'd you get that?"

He regarded me for a moment before speaking. "Stole it." His voice was cold and unsteady, as though he was speaking from a great distance away.

"Is it for your cell?" I spoke more quietly now, matching his tone.

"No." He chuckled. "But it'll cause a bit of chaos when the guards realize it's missing."

"What's it for?"

Opal slipped it up his sleeve and gave me an innocent smile. "What's what for?"

It was only after the guard left that I realized he was trying to hide the key.

"Ever thought of stealing something useful?" Kampê asked, bracing her elbows on the table.

"I have. It sounds boring. I'd rather steal useless things; forks, pencils, chalk, spare keys..." He trailed off and shrugged, his smile changing, becoming sharper. "Doesn't make a difference if they're gone but drives people mad when they realize they're missing something."

"Entertaining," she countered, waving her hand, "but ultimately a waste of talent." She leaned back in her chair.

Her hair was the color of butter, and her eyes were a striking emerald green. There was an unnerving stillness to her, like a snake about to strike, and her eyes were chillingly calm, cold, and calculating. Her features were sharp and narrow and dark, beautiful in an inhuman way. She bore an uncanny resemblance to Fas and was also the girl who had taunted me before, the one with the see-through green tank top and emerald pendant.

Looking at her, I pondered for a moment how much trouble I'd get in for starting a fight with another inmate.

"You think so," was all Opal said before lapsing back into purposeful silence.

Kampê turned her attention on me. "So…" She spoke leisurely, as if we had all the time in the world, and stirred her oatmeal. "You're new here, what are your thoughts so far?"

I shrugged, not meeting her gaze. "It's okay."

"It's okay," she repeated. She flicked her hair over her shoulder and pushed herself forward to get a better look at me, unslinging her arm from the back of the chair. "It's. Okay. Do you know where we are?" She asked it as though it were a dangerous question.

"Prison?"

"So you at least sort of know what's going on. Right?" She was smirking now, playing with me. "Learn anything interesting while you were still back at home?"

"Home?" I wanted to get into it with her *so badly*, but I pressed my lips together and resolved to say as few words as possible.

"You know, the Raising Center? Ooh, were you on the troublemaker's floor? You seem like the kind of person who would be on the troublemaker's floor." The seventh floor of the Raising Center was dedicated to the worst-behaved children of each generation. My room, room 737, was on the seventh floor. "You know, I always like it when we get a nice surprise— someone who stayed under the radar

163

their whole lives, but when you open them up, they're all sparkly and full of color, get it? Less predictable that way."

She knew she was getting under my skin. She *knew* it. I had to remind myself of that; it was the only thing that kept me from reacting.

Kampê grasped my arm with a surprising amount of gentleness, observing the sharp lines of red welts on my arm. "Looks like it hurt. What did you do?"

"I got out."

"Out?" she asked, eyes flaring. "As in, *out of the jail cell?*"

I made a small, vague sound, and Kampê composed herself, resuming her disinterested expression.

"How."

Rose went very still next to me, scanning the rows of lunch tables. She put her spoon down and her eyes stopped wandering, fixing on a single point somewhere in the middle of the room; she narrowed her eyes, knuckles going white on the table.

"What are you doing?" I kept my voice low, uncertain of whether to interrupt.

"Hold on," she whispered. Her fingers started tapping on the table, forming what almost seemed like patterns. Then she let out a tiny gasp and stopped. There was a hand on her shoulder.

"Come with me," the guard said, her sleek black hair pulled into a short ponytail.

Rose took a deep breath. Met the woman's eyes. Swallowed. Then she said, very simply: "No."

"Excuse me?" She reached for something, but Rose held up her hand.

"I will not be coming with you. I hope you can understand."

The guard's mouth went slack, eyes clouding over, before she blinked, nodded, and left.

"What did you just *do?*" I hissed.

Rose shook her head— she'd gone a few shades paler— and stared at her plate for the rest of breakfast.

CHAPTER 24

I was assigned to laundry duty. White tiled floors, gray walls. The room seemed to stretch on forever, lined with washing machines and driers. I had to sort the prison uniforms: day (gray), night (black), laundry (blue), kitchen (white), janitor's duty (orange).

Divide each pile into manageable loads, and then put each into the numerous washing machines. Depending on how large each load was, I would put a certain amount of detergent in each machine.

If it was a white load, I'd add bleach. When they were done, I'd put a new load into the washing machines and put the old load in the dryer. While I waited for each load to finish, I would fold the other loads as flawlessly as possible and then place each pile of clothes carefully into baskets that were redistributed among the inmates.

I spent the entire day in that laundry room, even though there were at least twenty other people working with me.

Thirty loads, five bleach stains, and ten stinging fingers later, I was done, having missed lunch and dinner.

My wounds were sore, my hands dry and cracked from too much contact with the detergent and water, and my skin had split near my cuticles and on my knuckles. In addition, I was starving, so hungry I couldn't focus. I'd barely touched my breakfast earlier, thinking it wise, but I regretted it now. It was awful.

My dreams were violent. Flashes of red and black and death and destruction, the scent of salt-kissed air winding through it all.

I was going to kill someone. Something. Everyone. Everyone deserved to die. Everyone deserved to experience the same pain I had experienced.

When I woke up, I went to attendance, fought to stay awake for breakfast, and then I was sent to cooking duty.

The air was hazy with steam and heavy with various smells. It was suffocating, and the space was tinted red. Smoke clogged my throat and pores and made my eyes water. Tiles lined the walls and floor, in a pattern that made me want to vomit.

The materials we had to use must've been leftovers from the actual Conurbation, and the food we created was sparse and messy. I tried to keep the kitchen uniform as clean as possible, thinking of the poor souls assigned to laundry duty.

I actually had time to eat lunch and dinner, but I had to do it in the kitchen. The kitchen's bathroom.

Still, food was better than no food.

The guards crowded close to me, monitoring my behavior closely. I was a convict now, a criminal. Then again, we all were.

But no matter how awful things got, I refused to complain, determined to keep my head down.

That day ended the same way the day before had, with me collapsing on my bed.

"You've been controlling yourself," Fas noted, swinging into a sitting position. "It seems to be working. They haven't been able to punish you for anything, despite your..." He struggled to find the right word before settling for the honest one, "despite your temper."

I gave him an irritated look, trying to get comfortable on the cot.

"I want you to go to the bathroom tomorrow after breakfast," he said, "and I want you to stay there. A handful of the others will find similar locations, and the rest will go to their duties as usual. We're going to get out of here."

I twisted to look at him.

"So," I tried to suppress my emotions. "You're going to do it."

"Yes."

"Okay," I said quietly. "Try not to die."

He smiled at me for the first time in a long time, flashing straight white teeth.

I didn't.

CHAPTER 25

The moment I finished breakfast, I slipped into the restroom stall, the lock clicking as I turned it to the side. I closed the lid to the toilet and sat down. The tiles were dirty white, and the fluorescent light flickered, on the verge of burning out. I lifted my legs and braced them against the blue-gray door.

Every single inmate here was either going to escape or die.

Every single one.

It was a mercy, I told myself, a mercy.

"Raven?" This voice was unmistakably Kitty's; it had the same sharp nasal tones, the same roughness around the edges.

"Yeah." I exhaled. She was alive. "Hi, Kitty."

"Yo," Jackie murmured. My thighs were starting to burn, sitting with my legs braced awkwardly against the door.

"Shut up." Kampê. I rolled my eyes.

Footsteps sounded outside and I stopped breathing, feeling my muscles lock. *Think*, I snapped at myself. *Think. Don't let this overwhelm your sense of reason.*

There was a plan; there were orders, orders I had to follow, would gladly follow, just this one last time. I had to try and focus on that.

"Steal as much food and as many clothes as possible," Fas had ordered last night. *"Not enough to weigh yourself down."* So I had, and now one of the laundry bags rested in my lap, the cord that kept it tied shut wound around my wrist.

This morning in laundry duty, I'd slipped off to the bathroom with a laundry bag stuffed up my shirt. Nonperishable goods and knives were exchanged for clothes and bags. And then I'd waited.

The guards hadn't even tried to keep their voices down last night, reporting the details of the next few days. Mass trials, nonstop from dawn till dusk. All verdicts would be final.

It was die today or die tomorrow.

Die on our own terms, as Fas had said, or die at the hands of our enemy.

I counted my breaths, keeping them shallow, keeping them silent.

Just a ways away, people started yelling, an alarm went off, and the lights went out.

That was our cue.

My feet padded silently in the dark, the pack slung over my back. This was nothing if not coordinated. Everyone knew what to do, except for the guards. But curiously, I didn't encounter a single person.

I tripped over something and stumbled once before continuing on my way.

Left. Left. Right. Straight. Right. Left. Right. Right. Straight. Left.

I was a machine, programmed to follow the instructions I had been given. My limbs moved on their own, the emergency sirens blaring in time with my heartbeat. Each breath came in heaving gasps, any pain I'd felt before gone, gone to this beautiful abyss of pure survival instinct.

Another second passed and the sirens faded into background noise as the other sounds came into sharp detail. Until I could hear people running corridors away.

Until I could hear my blood roaring through my veins. *Alive.* Almost seventeen, and I was alive. I was powered by the urge to live, and the urge to *get the hell out.*

It was dark, but all of a sudden I could see almost perfectly, could see the exact place I was supposed to remove the tile on the floor. The exit was almost impossible to reach, but this...

Yes, this would do just fine. I knelt, digging my fingers into the grout. The slate was indeed loose, but my nails broke all the same. I grit my teeth and pulled it out of its place, eyeing the ladder with distaste.

I didn't have time to be squeamish or picky.

But that didn't mean I had to like this.

The rungs were rusted and broken in places, each one in a crude 'U' shape. As I slipped my hand onto the first one, I shuddered. It was slimy.

And then I was moving again. My hands hooked on the rungs below and I swung each foot down as well until I saw the murky water below and jumped off, landing with a muffled splash. I couldn't contain my cringe, at my sloppiness, at the stench of the water, at the sodden insides of the shoes I wore.

That was when I saw the other people, running ahead of me.

Go. I had to go.

So I went, heaving myself onto the narrow catwalk on the side of the tunnel and sprinting. I slipped on the grimy bricks and almost fell into the water, but I recovered in time to keep going. I was getting tired now, slowing down as the adrenaline faded, but I didn't stop.

I headed down the left tunnel, running as fast as I could, streams of people joining me.

And the ground opened just in front of me, a drop that went straight down into nothingness. My heart skipped a beat.

No one else hesitated, each of them launching into the shaft with grim determination etched into every line in their faces. Only I was still as everyone else rushed around me, staring at the hole.

Go, breathed a different voice inside of me, an ancient voice that smelled like salt-laced wind.

I backed up one step, then another, glancing over my shoulder. And then I hurtled forward, my feet a blur beneath me, before throwing myself in.

The drop wasn't very far, but the way I landed sent spikes of pain up and down my leg, which gave out beneath me. Cursing, I dragged myself upright, scraping my fingertips on the bricks before leaning down to examine my throbbing ankle.

It was nothing, I told myself, using the wall to help me walk, just a sprain.

The back of my shirt was drenched, droplets of water showering my front. My hair was soaking wet, whipping my face.

It would take weeks for me to feel clean.

But I eased out of the shaft, setting my feet on the ground. There was a small platform here, with a set of stairs leading down to a shadowy pier. It was made of rusted metal and ancient wood that splintered at the water's every touch. Boats were tied to one of the supports.

I limped into the one closest to me, sliding into a fetal position next to Jackie.

All we needed now was for someone to release the boats.

It wasn't long before there was a scuffling sound from inside the shaft. I opened my eyes and waited, watching the dark void between the scrubbed-out graffiti on the walls.

A tall figure leaned in the exit, and I tensed. He had his hand over his face, his entire body shaking.

As he got closer, I realized he was glowing. Literally glowing— his visible eye was a brilliant turquoise, a spiderweb of veins lit blue beneath his skin. The hand covering his face was engulfed in aquamarine flames; as was the one hanging limply by his side.

He staggered forward, legs giving out as he landed on the pier, and dragged himself the rest of the way. Something glinted in his hand— a knife.

A bloody one.

He sliced the ropes that bound us to the pier and dragged himself onto our boat before slumping over.

I was the first to move, shaking his shoulders and pulling him up onto the seat. The motor started and we lurched into motion.

The left side of his face was ruined beyond repair. All that was left was the smoldering remains of a caved-in cheek, a temple, the corner of a lip. Part of his neck seemed to have been burned as well. His wrist was bent at an awkward angle, a swollen lump where one of his ribs would be. A gash tore down from his collarbone to his stomach, ripping through the fabric of his shirt, but the wound was *blue.*

Other, similar injuries slashed their way down his arms and legs, both knees skinned, a trickle of cobalt leaking from his ear. Blue liquid oozed down his face, glowing like his eyes were.

His lashes fluttered and his gaze darted to me, irises flaring gold before he passed out. His hair was black with faded blue tips, shaved except for a mohawk, combed to the side—

"What?" I touched his face. It didn't make any sense. But— it did.

I could see it now; in the shape and color of his eyes, in the feline stillness, in his slender frame, in his rare, faint smiles. In fact, now that I could see it, I couldn't *unsee* it.

Somehow this boy was Fas, but somehow, he was also Shadow.

His face— that was beyond repair. Better to clean the wound now and keep him from bleeding out. My hands tingled, pins and needles pricking my palms as my blood heated, my heart beating faster, that strange, foreign power itching to be released.

No. I clenched and unclenched my fingers, lips moving in a language I didn't know, warding off whatever strange power manifested in my veins.

"Does anyone here have any Medical experience?" I asked, my voice coming out strained.

Jackie stood. "I'll get Kampê."

"She has to stay on her boat," Rose pointed out. "She's supposed to be in the front so she can show us where to go."

"This won't take long," Jackie said.

When she returned, Kampê with her, they both looked uncharacteristically pale.

Kampê saw Fas, half conscious and slumped against the side of the dingy, she raised her eyebrows. "Idiot," she said, but there was a note of worry in her voice.

Then she knelt next to him, running her hands up and down his body.

"Broken ribs," she mused. "Fractured arm. Sprained wrist. Internal bleeding. Torn bicep. Severe blood loss." My lips moved with each word, my fingers tapping together. "He's lucky he didn't sever his spinal cord. I'm going to have to stay on this boat to take care of it." She sighed through her nose. "Jadel knows where to go, put them in charge for now, and we'll switch places the next time we stop. Give me thirty minutes."

I nodded, only half listening.

Jackie left to give Kampê's orders to everyone else, and Kampê leaned back, glancing around, before grabbing one of the metal seats.

"What are you doing?" I asked this because she had begun to shake it, pulling it back and forth, til the screws loosened and it started to come off.

"Shut up." She kicked the seat and it fell to the ground. Then her hands began to glow.

Kampê cradled the rusted thing to her chest, fingers lighting up until her bones blazed a molten gold and the metal started to heat up.

Slowly, steadily, it melted, and Kampê was holding a lump of smoldering liquid. She molded it, playing with it like it was clay, and before long she was holding a mask.

I watched him for a few minutes, watched the mask pressed to his face, watched him stir, eyes opening for a moment before closing once more. He made a small noise of protest.

"This is your fault, idiot." Kampê's eyes narrowed. "If you'd be more careful, I wouldn't have to put hot metal on your face. Sorry."

Fas didn't answer.

The river burbled serenely, hissing and sloshing. It was suffocating in the dark, the only thing piercing through was the weak light coming from where Kampê was working. The damp odor of rotting wood clogged my nose, an archway of stone serving as a ceiling of this ages-old sewage system.

Our boat sliced through the waves, the motor purring in the background.

And I watched as his hair changed, cropping closer to his head and darkening, the angle of his face changing ever so slightly, until it was Shadow, not Fas, who I stared at.

I don't know when I fell asleep.

CHAPTER 26

When my eyes opened, only Jackie was awake, monitoring the engine. She saw me and cracked a halfhearted grin before returning to her vigil.

Kampê was still on our boat, curled up in the fetal position. Her head leaned on Fas's shoulder. He was asleep, too, head propped up on his hands. Whatever glamour he'd used was back, displaying the leader I had come to know, rather than the quiet, steady presence that accompanied me in the night. The side of his face and neck were now...

Like his hand.

Metal and plastic plates slid into one another, smooth and sleek, every curve on his face replicated so perfectly that, had it not been a shining silver color, I would have been convinced it was the real thing. I didn't know what Kampê had done, but it was flawless.

The fingers on his left hand hovered less than a centimeter away from his cheek, as though he had fallen asleep running his fingers over it, trying to understand. I looked away from the horrible gashes that remained. Those would scar.

"The engine's dying," Jackie mumbled, rubbing her eyes. Indeed, the large black box at the end of the boat was sputtering and coughing. Fas stirred.

"It's old," he said, rising on unsteady legs and crossing to her. He pounded on it once, twice, with enough force to leave a dent, but it worked.

It must have been sometime in the morning, but the tunnels were so, so dark and...

"There's a light!" I cried, lunging to the front of the boat, seizing the sides for support and ignoring the sprays of water that slapped my face and filled my mouth.

"What?" Jackie looked much more awake now.

"Look!" I tugged her up to where I sat, pointing towards the growing shafts of light in the distance.

"Oh my God! Oh my God, we're finally going to get out of here!" She squeezed me in a hug, tears streaming down her face.

"We're finally going to get out of here," she repeated weakly. "I can't—"

Jackie didn't get to finish her sentence. A Conurbation soldier, hiding along the side of the boat, had grabbed her leg and begun to drag her overboard. She cried out, seizing my wrist, dark eyes wide and desperate.

Before I could even think, I was tugging Jackie back towards us, reaching into her bag, pulling out a knife.

Jackie was sobbing, her grip beginning to loosen on my arm.

I pressed my lips together. "Duck," I said, and threw the knife.

It wasn't me.

It wasn't me.

It wasn't me.

I looked away as the knife found its mark, expecting him to scream. He didn't. Kampê was awake now, pulling Jackie close.

I bit my knuckle and slid to the ground.

His blood was on my hands.

I had killed him.

It felt different, I reflected. It *was* different, when you were the killer instead of the bystander.

A hand touched my shoulder. Fas.

Don't pull away. He didn't. I leaned my head on his shoulder

"You're gonna be okay," he said into my hair. "It's always hard, the first time."

The light illuminated the tunnel and I could suddenly make out the glossy black surface of the river, the stone bricks, the narrow catwalks on the sides of the river for the sewer workers.

Then I could see distant shapes as my eyes adjusted, curving slopes, endless horizon, misty dawn. It was breathtaking.

I gasped, grabbing Fas's arm. The river emptied out into a waterfall.

He laughed at me, turning me away from the exit to wrap his arms around my waist. I became something else entirely. "Don't look," he advised, leaning his forehead against mine, "it helps." I nodded and closed my eyes.

Then, almost before I knew what I was doing, I leaned in, he pulled me closer, and our lips met as the boat went over the edge and into freefall.

I grabbed the back of his head, forcing him closer before he could pull away. His hands curled in my hair, his teeth clamped down on my tongue and I cried out, but I didn't move. It was survival, it was desperation, it was heaven.

Some part of me became obscurely aware that I had a crippling fear of heights, but I didn't care, I couldn't care; there was no room for fear.

How many times had he looked at me, either in this form or as Shadow, as though I simply didn't understand?

Now I understood.

Now I got it.

And then we slammed into the water; everyone was dislodged, crashing into cold waves. Somehow, I felt that strange rippling of energy surround me once again, seconds before I struck the water and died.

Beneath the surface the water was freezing, colder than it had been at the top.

A part of me was aware that the boat landed on top of me and I should have been crushed, but all I could see were the bubbles of air rolling up to the surface, cool green shafts of light slicing through the water, an underwater landscape. Some instinct kicked in and I held my breath without fully knowing why.

It was incredible.

But I didn't know how to swim. So I thrashed for a moment, chest constricting, panic setting in, before managing to kick upwards.

Rose ran her fingers through her soaking-wet hair, pulling her legs underneath her from the shore. Her face bore a rare scowl. "It's going to be all straight and ugly now," she complained, leaning against Jackie's shoulder.

Apollo rolled his eyes. "Oh, God forbid it be *straight.*" He was gripping the side of one of the boats, struggling to stay above the surface.

"You can't scratch water," Kampê informed him. "It's a liquid."

Apollo offered a vulgar gesture in response.

I slowed my kicking to save energy and glanced around.

The lake was surrounded by a pale-sand-and-pebble beach, several boulders jutting from the shore and the water.

Sunlight speared through the clouds in shafts; the sky was impossibly blue.

Trees rose in the distance, tall enough to poke holes in the sky. I had never seen so many greens in my life— the trees, the bushes, the grass, the moss, the algae.

The water sparkled like glass, so clear I could see the sandy floor.

A gentle breeze rustled in the brush. Mountains thrust their twisting spires through the bowels of the earth, piercing the atmosphere and slicing through the clouds.

The air was cold compared to the desert, crisper than I was used to, and the songs and shrieks of various animals echoed from the forest.

"I hope you drown," Rose said cheerfully, responding to Apollo's earlier remark.

"Go die in a hole."

"Aren't you two just the cutest thing," Kampê drawled, stretching out lazily on a rock. Her eyes slid shut, sunlight painting her golden. She was unfairly pretty, I thought, watching the light dance on her cheekbones. "I could stay here forever."

"Awesome. I feel so happy for you," I said. "I don't know how to swim. Can I have some help please?"

"Try hard, I believe in you." Kampê didn't open her eyes.

"I don't," Rose offered.

"How did you even get over there?" I was getting tired and a tiny bit scared, if I was honest with myself.

"We swam." Kampê's tone was bored, but her face was the picture of malicious amusement. "Try it."

I opened my mouth and closed it again, choosing to save my breath.

"Here." Fas came up next to me, treading with ease. "Grab on."

I wrapped my arms around his waist and rested my cheek on his back, letting him pull me to shore.

"You should have let her figure it out on her own," Kampê said mildly as Fas helped me to my feet.

He shook his head. "And if she drowned?"

"Well, that's her problem, not yours." The corner of her mouth quirked upward.

"Go help set up camp. See if you can hunt anything. I'm going to help everyone else out of the water." For a moment, I thought Kampê would argue, but, at the look on her brother's face, she did as she was told.

Two people had died. Three more were injured.

We worked in silence, grabbing bags and checking if anything was worth salvaging. The clothes we'd brought with us were hung from branches to dry, the knives laid out on rocks, and the food wrapped in the laundry bags and tucked away in the trees.

Some of the cans had burst, scattering their contents across the lake, and some of the food was just ruined. What we had was what we had, now that we were alone and far away from the only place we'd come to see as home.

CHAPTER 27

The fallen tree I sat on was covered in moss. It was soft, with a rich, earthy smell to it. Interlocking patterns of rough bark wove together on the trunk, secrets written in a tongue I didn't understand.

"Like in the greenhouses," Rose mused as I fingered the plush green leaves. She had several herbs and roots scattered across a stone slab and was chopping at them with one of the knives we still had.

Fas was sitting on a boulder, glancing up at the Barrier and back to the stone before him, scratching numbers on it with a burnt stick. He was leaning against one of the jagged spires of rock, curled into it comfortably as though he had grown up in this clearing, shoes kicked off several feet away.

I hadn't decided how I felt about him lying yet, or whether I'd forgiven him.

We were broken up into several small circles of people gathered around flaming piles of dead wood. Kampê had set most of them alight. How she did it, I had no idea, but I was glad for the warmth.

"Does anyone have any salt?" Rose asked. "It won't taste good without it."

Kampê stalked across the circle and wordlessly deposited a handful of white crystals on the slab. I watched her as she turned on her heel and left.

"Where did she even *get* that?" I muttered, earning a venomous smile.

"What's in it?" Crystal inquired, craning to get a better look and mostly ignoring me.

"Hmm," Rose glanced around at the gathered food. "Wild potatoes, taro, basil, some wild carrots, other stuff, and wild strawberries for dessert."

"*Other stuff?*" Kampê repeated, rolling her eyes.

"What's *dessert?*" I asked.

Kampê burst into harsh, cruel laughter, throwing her head back in a way that was almost serpentine. I wanted the answer to my question, but I didn't want to ask again.

After the soup was made, Rose found that she had not thought far enough ahead to consider what the soup would be going in. Eventually, after a slight freakout, she just poured it into the leftover cans and told people to be careful not to cut their lips.

The broth was a greenish yellow color, with chopped vegetables floating in it. Steam curled off the top of the liquid, and it smelled familiar; like Thursday soup suppers in the Conurbation.

It did not taste like Thursday soup suppers; it had a distinct, earthy taste, with alternating bits of sweet and salt.

Rose sat down next to me. "Have you seen Apollo?" she asked. "Because it's very unusually quiet and nice and non-nihilistic here."

"You're bored, aren't you?" I glanced at her. "Since you don't have anyone to argue with?"

"A little bit, yeah."

"I think he got hurt when we fell down the waterfall." Fas had been missing for a good hour now; I suspected he'd gone to help.

"Do you think he'll die?" she asked. "I hope he dies. I really, *really* hope he dies."

"You are just a little ray of sunshine," Jackie said, pulling her knees up to her chest, "aren't you?"

"Why, yes I am. Thank you for noticing."

Kampê rolled her eyes for what had to be the hundredth time, growing hostile when she saw the look on my face.

"Is there an issue?"

"Apparently," I said under my breath.

She stood and crossed over to me, resting one knee next to my leg. "What seems to be the problem?"

"Maybe you should tell me."

"Why?" Her voice told me that she knew exactly why.

"I mean, I'm not the one who—" I caught myself. "No reason. Never mind."

"That's what I thought," she said, and walked off into the trees, announcing that she was "going to find Fas."

Opal had been gathering the cans as people finished their soup, cleaning them in a nearby stream, filling them again, and redistributing them. He had stopped now and was talking to Rose, sitting cross-legged in front of her.

"I think you've met Raven," Rose was saying.

"Sort of."

"She's right over there." Rose pointed at me, and Opal turned and waved, offering an awkward smile. I noticed that his pinky finger was missing right down to the joint above the knuckle and shuddered.

The Liberation Center.

Where Defects went to die.

"Hi," Opal said. "I don't think we've formally met."

"Not formally."

"You're new."

I nodded.

He laughed. "You're in for a load of fun the next few years."

"Don't listen to him," Jackie said.

"You shouldn't," he said seriously. "Because I'm crazy." He smiled again at the exasperated noise Jackie made. "At least," he went on, "that's what I've heard."

I pressed my lips together before allowing myself a grin.

"Okay." Rose patted my shoulder. "Bedtime."

"Where?"

"On the ground. It's comfy, I promise."

I used to stay up all night to watch the stars. My Raisers found out and took me to a Medical, who gave me several medications that I always forgot to take. Then there was the knockout gas. I was given several warnings before they tried to give it to me, and when they did,

I broke the equipment. Still, I started going to bed earlier, and they stopped giving me the medications; a compromise.

Now I stared up at the sky, waiting as my gaze adjusted and more and more stars became visible. I traced the patterns until my eyes grew heavy; I rolled over and fell asleep.

I dreamt I was running. I didn't know where I was or where I was going; the only word that came to mind was *away*. A dusty road stretched endlessly in both directions, an expansive desert on either side of me.

There were four monsters. Three were awake, one was sleeping; one came from the east, one from the west, one from the north, and one from the sky.

Then, as I ran, I became aware of someone running right next to me. They shifted closer and closer until they almost touched me.

Karen, they whispered. *Wake up.*

I flinched.

"It's alive!" There was the sensation of fingers tugging my hair near my scalp, and after a moment I realized Rose was running her hands through my hair. "How'd you sleep? We're leaving, by the way."

"Alright," I said, both in response to her question and what she'd said about us leaving.

She offered her hand, tucking her hair behind her ear— her earlier prediction had come true; her bright pink hair was pin straight. "Upsy daisy."

I yawned and ran a hand through my own hair. I stopped when I found a knot in the back.

"You two look kind of similar with your hair straight," Jackie remarked, coming up behind us and slinging one arm around each of our shoulders. She tugged on our arms and spun us around, so Rose and I were both facing her. "See? Yeah, I think it's, like, the shape of your eyes, maybe?"

Rose laughed and picked up Jackie's hand, playing with her fingers. "Nothing else you can think of?"

"I mean, I could go *on,* but we *do* have to go. That's actually what I'm here to talk about; it's leaving time, children, get your things."

I picked up my bag, allowing one last glance towards the Barrier.

I was never going to have to see it again after today.

"What is that?" Jackie was asking.

What is— oh.

A large, white *something* was ascending into the air, roaring as it did so.

"Uh," Fas said, coming up beside me. He looked afraid for the first time since I'd met him. "They have a helicopter. Go."

"What's a—"

"Go." He pushed my arm; Rose grabbed me by the wrist and dragged me along.

I felt the surge of adrenaline in my veins, but it didn't make me go any faster; it made me panic.

"What is that thing?" I asked, starting to feel nauseous.

"Bad," Rose shouted over the noise. I nodded, but my chest tightened. "Listen, Raven—" Her sentence came in short, breathy parts; she yanked me sideways. "I know... it's confusing, I promise I'll... explain later... but we have to get out of here... because those things are *fast*."

People were scattering in all directions. Someone rammed into my side, almost knocking me down, but Rose pulled me to my feet again and we kept going, heading towards the dark green trees.

Someone screamed something about a bomb.

Rose cursed and stopped in the middle of the crowd, whipping her head around, trying to figure out where to go.

There was a muffled *boom* followed by a chorus of shrieks.

The entire clearing was enveloped in smoke; within moments I was gasping for breath. Each breath was like inhaling shards of glass,

195

but still my legs pushed me forward, struggling to put distance between me and whatever lay behind. Between water and flame.

Between life and certain death.

Fiery heat pulled at me, strangled me, choked me, burned me. My ears were ringing; I couldn't hear anything.

Fas shoved me along, yelling in my ear as my vision grew hazy.

"... going to carry..."

He wrapped my arm around his shoulder, but I shoved him away in a panic, stumbling a few more steps before falling to the ground.

And then I felt the wall of fire slam into me. My body screamed in burning agony.

I lurched forward on all fours, hitting my head on the ground.

Darkness was all I knew.

E P I L O G U E

The wasteland stretched endlessly below her; though nature had started to reclaim the landscape.

Centuries of planning, thousands of years of waiting, and they were about to ruin it all.

The being at the center of the room ran her hands through her thick black hair.

It would be fine. She would handle it; she always did. This was all a game, she just needed to follow the rules and she would win.

Astris smoothed her dress, narrowing her eyes. Just a game, although there was a lot at stake. She was forbidden from directly interfering with human interactions for completely arbitrary reasons—something foolish she'd done hundreds of thousands of years ago—

but all her pieces were in place, she only needed to be sure she played them right.

Once all was said and done, things would do one of two things: go back to normal, everyone secluded in their little cities, forgetting where they came from, losing track of their original purposes— she'd hated that gods-damned agreement from its hideous conception— or it would all be destroyed and everyone would be forced to get along. She liked that option much better.

Alright, Tyros, she thought, pressing her lips into a thin line, *your move.*

UNCHAIN SNEAK PEEK

"Take her to Decontamination."

It hurt.

It hurt, it hurt, *it hurt.*

There was a snapping sound and the lights flickered, trapping the world in darkness. Warm, sweet darkness.

Gone after a moment, and the light returned, along with a pounding headache.

I moaned. My hand fisted, eyes screwing up as I strained against whatever binds held me in place. *Dark.* I wanted it to be dark.

"Shh." There was a hand on my head, stroking my hair. "It's okay."

Dark.

"Dark," I mumbled. My voice was pathetic, raspy.

"I'm sorry, we have to keep it this way."

"Dark."

"She's feverish," came another voice. "We're losing her."

"Dark." I was crying, pleading. "Dark." I needed the word, what was the word?

"What is she saying?"

"Dark!" I was screaming now, yanking against my binds. *"Dark!"*

And there it was. The word I needed.

Ófojr. Again. Again.

There was a pause, fearful silence.

The lights went out.

But this was a different kind of darkness.

It filled every corner, slipped between my shoulder blades and curled around my ear. It came from me.

The Medicals were screaming, but I couldn't hear.

It was silent.

ABOUT THE AUTHOR

Kayleigh Gallagher is a teen author, perfectionist, and stressed-out high schooler. She wrote her first "book" back in fourth grade, and her parents bought into this unrealistic dream and helped her "publish" it. The first draft of *Defy* was written in 2016, and it was just sixty-six pages long. Now, of course, it's much longer, and it's the first in a series.

INSTAGRAM: @SO_MANY_OCS

PINTEREST: @SOMANYOCS

FACEBOOK: KAYLEIGH GALLAGHER- AUTHOR

WEBSITE: <u>*KAYLEIGH GALLAGHER ON GOOGLE*</u>

<u>*SITES*</u>

Made in the USA
San Bernardino, CA
04 May 2020